George MacDonald

Violin Songs

George MacDonald

Violin Songs

ISBN/EAN: 9783744767293

Printed in Europe, USA, Canada, Australia, Japan

Cover: Foto ©Andreas Hilbeck / pixelio.de

More available books at **www.hansebooks.com**

VIOLIN SONGS

By GEORGE MAC DONALD, LL.D.

A NEW EDITION

LONDON
CHATTO & WINDUS
1897

WORKS OF FANCY AND IMAGINATION

By GEORGE MACDONALD, LL.D.

VOL. III.

A NEW EDITION

LONDON

CHATTO & WINDUS

1897

CONTENTS.

SONGS OF THE DAYS AND NIGHTS:

A BOOK OF DREAMS 115

ROADSIDE POEMS :—

VIOLIN SONGS.

VIOLIN SONGS.

HOPE DEFERRED.

SUMMER is come again. The sun is bright,
  And the soft wind is breathing. Airy joy
Is sparkling in thine eyes, and in their light
My soul is shining. Come; our day's employ
Shall be to revel in unlikely things,
In gayest hopes, fondest imaginings,
And make-believes of bliss. Come, we will talk
Of waning moons, low winds, and a dim sea,
Till this fair summer, deepening as we walk,
Has grown a paradise for you and me.

But ah, those leaves!—it was not summer's
    mouth
Breathed such a gold upon them. And look
    there—
That beech how red! See, through its boughs
    half-bare,
How low the sun lies in the mid-day south !—
'Tis but a wandering memory that hath shone
Back from the summer mourning to be gone.
See, see the dead leaves falling! Hear thy
    heart,
Which, changing ever as seasons come and go,
Takes in the changing world its mournful part,
Return a sigh, an echo sad and low
To the faint, half inaudible sound
With which the leaf goes whispering to the
    ground !
O love, the winter lieth at the door—
Behind the winter, age and something more.

Come round me, dear hearts. All of us will
 hold
Each one encompassed : we are growing old ;
And if we be not as a ring enchanted
Around each heart, with love to keep it gay,
The young, who claim the joy that haunted
Our visions once, will push us far away
Into the desolate regions, dim and gray,
Where the sea moans, and hath no other cry,
The cloud is mist, and hath no rain of tears,
The past sinks swallowed in a pit of years,
And hopes and joys both careless pass us by;
But if all each do keep,
The rising tide of youth will sweep
Around us with its laughter-joyous waves,
As ocean fair some palmy island laves,
To loneliness heaved slow from out the deep ;
And our lost youth keep hovering like the breath
Round one that sleeps, and sleepeth not to death.

Bound thus together, on to parted graves,
The sundered doors into one palace home,
Stumbling through age's thickets we will go,
Faltering but faithful—willing to lie low,
Willing to part, not willing to deny
The lovely past, where all the futures lie.

Oh ! if thou be—called of the living lord,
Not of the dead—lo ! by that self-same word,
Thou art not lord of age, but lord of youth ;
Because there is no age, in sooth,
Beyond its passing shows :
A mist o'er life's dimmed lantern grows ;
But when the glass is broken, lo, the light
That knows not youth nor age,
That fears no darkness nor the rage
Of windy tempests—burning still more bright
Than when glad youth was all about,
And summer winds were out !

DEATH.

WHEN in the bosom of the eldest night
This body lies, cold as a sculptured rest ;
When through its shaded windows comes no light,
And its pale hands are folded on its breast—

How shall I fare, who had to wander out,
When mysteries around me heave and toss ?
Shall I peer vague-eyed, fearful, all about,
Or turn and brood o'er faces white with loss ?

Depart slow-floating, like a mist, away,
First o'er the city murmuring beneath ;
Next o'er the trees and fields, all-thoughtful, stray,
To find the mountain and the lonely heath ?

Or will a darkness, o'er material shows
Descending, hide them from the spirit's sight ;
As from the sun a blotting radiance flows
Across the stars that shone all through the night ;

And so the spirit hang entranced, alone,
Like one in an exalted opium-dream—
Soft-flowing time, insisting space, o'erblown,
With form and colour, tone and touch and gleam ;

Thought only waking—thought that may not own
The lapse of ages, or the change of spot ;
Whose doubt is cast on what it counted known,
Whose faith is fixed on what appeareth not?

Or, worn with weariness, shall we sleep until,
First life restored by long and dreamless rest,
Of God's oblivion having drunk our fill,
We wake his little ones, peaceful and blest?

I nothing know.   And wherefore should I
  know ?
God is ; I shall be ever in his sight.
Give thou me strength to labour well, and so
Do the day's work ere fall the coming nignt.

HARD TIMES.

I AM weary, and very lonely,
  And can but think—think.
If there were some water only
  That a spirit might drink—drink !
    And arise,
    With light in the eyes
And a crown of hope on the brow,
  To walk abroad in the strength of gladness,
  Not sit in the house benumbed with sadness—
    As now !

But, Lord, thy child will be sad—
  As sad as it pleases thee ;

Will sit, not seeking to be glad,

Till thou bid sadness flee ;

And drawing near

With a kind "good cheer,"

Awake the life in me.

IF I WERE A MONK, AND THOU WERT A NUN.

IF I were a monk, and thou wert a nun,
  Pacing it wearily, wearily,
From chapel to cell till day were done—
  Wearily, wearily—
How would it fare with these hearts of ours
That need the sunshine, and smiles, and flowers?

To prayer, to prayer, at the matins' call,
  Morning foul or fair !—
Words from the lips that drop and fall—
  Alas, no soaring prayer !
The chapel's roof, like the law in stone,
Caging the lark that up had flown.

Thou, in the glory of cloudless noon,
  The God-revealing,
Turning thy face from the boundless boon—
  Painfully kneeling ;
Or, in brown-shadowy solitude,
Bending thy head o'er the legend rude.

I, in a sad and lonely nook,
  Gloomily, gloomily,
Poring over some musty book,
  Thoughtfully, thoughtfully ;
Or painting quaint pictures of things of old
On the parchment-margin with purple and gold.

Perchance in slow procession to meet,
  Wearily, wearily,
In antique, narrow, high-gabled street,
  Wearily, wearily ;

Dark eyes lifted to mine, and then
Heavily sinking to earth again!

Sunshine and air ! bird-music and spring !
    Merrily, merrily !—
Back to its cell each weary thing,
    Wearily, wearily !
Hearts that are withered and dry and old,
Are most at home in the cloister cold.

Thou on thy knees ere the vespers' call,
    Wearily, wearily ;
I looking up on the darkening wall,
    Wearily, wearily ;
The chime so sweet to the boat at sea,
Listless and dead to thee and me !

Then for sleep a weary assay,
    On the lone couch wearily ;

Rising at midnight again to pray,
>   Wearily, wearily !
Ah, through the dark those eyes look in !
Away ! away ! 'tis a thought of sin !

And at last, when thou wert passing away,
>   Dreamily, dreamily—
Thy worn tent fluttering in dim decay,
>   Sleepily, sleepily—
Over thee held the crucified Best,
But no warm cheek to thy cold cheek pressed !

And when this body were going its way,
>   Dreamily, dreamily—
Its gray head lying on ashes gray,
>   Sleepily, sleepily—
No woman-angel hovering above,
Ready to clasp me in deathless love !

But now, ah, now ! thy hand in mine,

　　Peacefully, peacefully ;

My arm around thee, my lips on thine,

　　Lovingly, lovingly—

Oh ! is not a better thing to us given

Than wearily going alone to heaven ?

MY HEART.

I.

NIGHT, with her power to silence day,
  Filled up my lonely room,
Quenching all sounds but one that lay
  Beyond her passing doom,
Where in his shed a workman gay
  Went on despite the gloom.

I listened, and I knew the sound,
  And the trade that he was plying ;
For backwards, forwards, bound and bound,
  A shuttle was flying, flying—
Weaving ever—till, all unwound,
  The weft go out with a sighing.

II.

As hidden in thy chamber lowest
    As in the sky the lark—
O mystic thing, thou working goest
    Without the poorest spark,
And yet light's garment round me throwest,
    Who else, as thou, were dark.

With body ever clothing me,
    Thou fillest me with light ;
I look, and lo the earth and sea,
    The sky's rejoicing height—
A woven glory, globed by thee
    Around my lonely night!

And when thy darkling labours fail,
    And thy shuttle moveless lies,
The whole will drop, like an untied veil
    From before a lady's eyes ;

Or, all night read, a finished tale,
  That in the morning dies.

III.

Yet not in vain dost thou unroll
  The stars, the world, the seas—
A mighty, wonder-painted scroll
  Of Patmos mysteries—
Thou mediator 'twixt my soul
  And better things than these !

Thy holy ephod bound on me,
  I am a gifted seer ;
For still in things thou mak'st me see,
  The unseen grows more clear ;
Still their indwelling Deity
  Speaks plainer in mine ear.

Oh, holy high the mission is
   Which thought to thinking brings !
Thy web, the nursing chrysalis
   Round Psyche's folded wings,
To them transfers the loveliness
   Of its inwoven things.

Yet joy when thou shalt cease to beat !—
   A greater heart beats on,
Whose rich brocade will follow fleet
   Thy last frail thread outrun—
A seamless-woven garment, meet
   To clothe a death-born son.

NEW ANGELS.

Of old, with goodwill from the skies—
  God's message to them given—
The angels came, a glad surprise,
  And went again to heaven.

But now the angels are grown rare—
  Needed no more as then :
Far lowlier messengers can bear
  God's goodwill unto men.

Each year, the snowdrops' pallid dawn
  Breaks from the earth below ;
Till, from the dark exulting drawn,
  The noon of roses glow.

The snowdrop first—the dawning grav ;
    Then out the roses burn !
They speak their word, grow dim—away
    To holy dust return.

Of oracles were little dearth,
    Should heaven continue dumb ;
From lowliest corners of the earth
    High messages will come.

Since in thy face, redeeming Lord,
    We saw the Father's kind,
We need not much his rarer word—
    Our eyes can read his mind.

TO MY SISTER

I.

OLD fables are not all a lie,
　That tell of wondrous birth,
Of Titan children, father Sky,
　And mighty mother Earth.

Yea, now are walking on the ground
　Sons of the mingled brood ;
Yea, now upon the earth are found
　Such daughters of the Good.

Earthborn, my sister, thou art still
　A daughter of the sky ;
Oh, climb for ever up the hill
　Of thy divinity.

To thee thy mother Earth is sweet,
    Her face to thee is fair ;
But thou, a goddess incomplete,
    Must climb the starry stair.

II.

Wouldst thou the holy hill ascend,
    And see the Father's face ?
To all his children humbly bend,
    And seek the lowest place.

Be like a cottage on a moor,
    A covert from the wind,
With burning fire and open door,
    And welcome free and kind.

Thus humbly doing on the earth
  What things the earthly scorn,
Thou shalt assert the lofty birth
  Of all the lowly born.

III.

Be then thy sacred womanhood
  A sign upon thee set,
A second baptism—understood—
  For what thou must be yet.

For, cause and end of all thy strife,
  And unrest as thou art—
Still stings thee to a higher life
  The Father at thy heart.

OH THOU OF LITTLE FAITH!

SAD-HEARTED, be at peace: the snowdrop lies
    Buried in sepulchre of ghastly snow ;
But spring is floating up the southern skies,
    And darkling the pale snowdrop waits below.

Let me persuade : in dull December's day
    We scarce believe there is a month of June ;
But up the stairs of April and of May
    The hot sun climbeth to the summer's noon.

Yet hear me : I love God, and half I rest.
    O better ! God loves thee, so all rest thou.
He is our summer, our dim-visioned Best ;—
    And in his heart thy prayer is resting now.

WILD FLOWERS.

BOUNTIFUL Primroses—

Whose hearts outspread peep from the soft leaves'
    care,

As from his mother's lap the little child

Who courts shy shelter from his own open air !

Hang-head Bluebell,

Bending like Moses' sister over Moses,

Heavy with secrets which thou dar'st not tell !

Fluttering-wild

Anemone, so well

Named of the wind, whereto, all free,

Thou yieldest helpless-wilfully,

With *Take me or leave me,*

Sweet Wind, I am thine own Anemone !

Thirsty forest Arum, ever dreaming

Of lakes in sunny wildernesses gleaming !

Fire-hearted Pimpernel,

Communing with some hidden well,

And secrets with the sun-god holding—

At fixed hour folding and unfolding !

How is it with you, children all,

When human children on you fall,

Gather you in eager haste,

Forget your beauty in their waste,

Fill and fill their full-filled hands ?

Goeth a tearing through your breast,

A fainting, melting of your bands ?

Do you know

When the spoilers near you come

By a shuddering in your gloom ?

For blind and deaf we think you are,

Hearing, seeing, near nor far :

Is it so ?

WILD FLOWERS.

Is it only ye are dumb ?
You alive at least I think,
Trembling almost on the brink
Of our lonely consciousness :
If it be so,
Take this comfort for your woe,
For the breaking of your rest,
For the tearing in your breast,
For the blotting of the sun,
For the death too soon begun,
For all else beyond redress,
For the thing ye cannot be—
That the children's wonder-springs
Bubble high at sight of you,
Lovely, lowly, common things—
More believing than they see,
When ye float into their view ;
That ye, bravely creeping out,
Smile away our manhood's doubt,

And our childhood's faith renew ;
And that we, with old age nigh,
Seeing you alive and well
Out of winter's crucible—
You who from the grave have crept,
Telling us ye only slept—
Think we die not, though we die.

Thus ye die not, though ye die—
Only yield your being up,
Like a nectar-holding cup :
Deaf, ye give to them that hear,
With a greatness lovely-dear ;
Blind, ye give to them that see—
Poor, but bounteous royally.

Lowly servants to the higher,
Burning upwards in the fire
Of Nature's endless sacrifice,
Thus in life's ascent ye rise ;
Thus you leave the earth behind,

And pass into the human mind,

Pass with it up into God,

Whence ye came down through the clod—

Pass, and find yourselves at home

Where but life can go and come;

Where all life is in its nest,

At holy one with awful Best.

SPRING SONG.

DAYS of old,
Ye are not dead, though gone from me;
Ye are not cold,
But like the summer-birds fled o'er some sea.
The sun brings back the swallows fast
O'er the sea :
When he cometh at the last,
The days of old come back to me.

SUMMER SONG.

"MURMURING, 'twixt a murmur and moan,
Many a tune in a single tone—
For every ear with a secret true—
The sea-shell wants to whisper to you."

"Yes—I hear it—far and faint,
Like thin-drawn prayer of drowsy saint ;
Like the muffled sounds of a summer rain ;
Like the rustle of dreams to a weary brain."

"By smiling lip and fixed eye,
You are hearing a song within the sigh :
The murmurer has curious ways—
Tell me, darling, the words it says."

"I hear a wind on a boatless main
Sigh like the last of a vanishing pain ;
On the dreaming waters dreams the moon :
But I hear no words in the doubtful tune."

"If it tell thee not that I love thee well,
'Tis a senseless, wrinkled, ill-curved shell :
If it be not of love, why sigh or sing ?
'Tis a common, mechanical, stupid thing."

"It whispers, it whispers, with prophet voice,
Of a peace that comes, of a granted choice ;
It speaks not a word of your love to me,
But it tells me I love you eternally."

AUTUMN SONG.

AUTUMN clouds are flying, flying
   O'er the waste of blue ;
Summer flowers are dying, dying,
   Late so lovely new.
Labouring wains are slowly rolling
   Home with winter grain ;
Holy bells are slowly tolling
   Over buried men.

Goldener light sets noon a sleeping
   Like an afternoon ;
Colder airs come stealing, creeping
   From the misty moon ;

D 9

And the leaves, of old age dying,
   Earthy hues put on ;
Out on every lone wind sighing
   That their day is gone.

Autumn's sun is sinking, sinking
   Down to winter's night ;
And our hearts are thinking, thinking
   Of the cold and blight ;
For our sun is slowly sliding
   Down the hill of might ;
And no moon is softly gliding
   Up the slope of night.

But the vanished corn is lying
   In rich golden glooms ;
In the churchyard, all the sighing
   Is above the tombs ;

And the flowers but wait the blowing
  Of a gentler wind :
Man waits not—through death's door going,
  Man leaves death behind.

Mourn not, then, bright hues that alter ;
  Let the gold turn gray ;
Feet though feeble still may falter
  Towards the coming day.
Brother, if thy sorrow lingers
  O'er some withered thing,
Mark at least that Autumn's fingers
  Paint in hues of Spring.

WINTER SONG.

THEY were parted then at last?
  Was it duty, or force, or fate?
Or only a wordy blast
  Blew-to the meeting-gate?

An old old story is this—
  A glance, a trembling, a sigh,
A gaze in the eyes, a kiss—
  Why will it *not* go by?

PICTURE SONGS.

I.

A PALE green sky is gleaming ;
  The steely stars are few ;
The moorland pond is steaming
  A mist of gray and blue.

Along the pathway lonely
  My horse is walking slow ;
Three living creatures only,
  We, and a far up crow !

The moon is hardly shaping
  Her circle in the fog ;
A brook half sings, escaping
  Its prison in the bog.

But in my heart are ringing
Rich tones of lofty song,
As one I know were singing
A sister-choir among.

II.

OVER a shining land—
   Once such a land I knew—
Over its sea and over its sand,
   The sky is all white and blue.

Its waves are kissing its shores,
   Murmuring on and ever ;
Its boats are green, and their timeful oars
   Flash out of the level river.

Oh to be there with thee,
   Wandering the shore, my love !
The shining sands and the sparkling sea !
   And the great bright sky above !

III.

THE autumn winds are sighing ·
   Over land and sea;
The autumn woods are dying
   Over hill and lea ;
And my heart is sighing, dying,
   Maiden, for thee.

The autumn clouds are flying
   Homeless over me ;
The nestless birds are crying
   In the naked tree ;
And my heart is flying, crying,
   Maiden, to thee.

The autumn sea is crawling
   Up the chilly shore ;
The thin-voiced firs are calling
   Ghostily evermore.
Maiden, maiden ! I am falling
   Dead at thy door.

IV.

THE waters are rising and flowing
　　Over the weedy stone—
Over it, over it going :
　　It is never gone.

Over it joys go sweeping :
　　'Tis there—the ancient pain ;
Yea, drowned in waves and waves of weeping,
　　It will rise again.

A DREAM SONG.

I DREAMED of a song—I heard it sung ;
In the ear that sleeps not, its music rung.
What were the words I could not tell,
Only the voice I heard right well,
Whose tones unearthly my spirit bound
In a calm delirium of mystic sound—
Floating where lonely Thought delights,
Placeless and silent, to drink the dew
That bathes the spirit from cloudy heights
The loftiest knowledge never knew.
A woman's voice woke echoes deep
That all day long in the spirit sleep,
In cavern or solitude, each apart,
Somewhere hid in the waiting heart—

A voice with a wild melodious cry
After something afar and high :
Sorrowful triumph, and hopeful strife,
And gainful death, and new-born life,
In every note of the prophet-song,
Made a tuneful prayer : O Lord, how long
Shall we groan and travail and faint and cry,
Ere the lovely sonship once draw nigh ?

SONGS OF THE DAYS AND NIGHTS.

SONGS OF THE DAYS AND NIGHTS.

SONGS OF THE SUMMER DAYS.

I.

GLORY on the chamber wall!
A glory in the brain!
Triumphant floods of glory fall
On heath, and wold, and plain.

The earth lies still in hopeless bliss ·
She has, and seeks no more;
Forgets that days come after this,
Forgets the days before.

Each ripple waves a flickering fire
  Of gladness, as it runs;
They laugh and flash, and leap and spire,
  And toss ten thousand suns.

But hark! low, in the world within,
  One sad æolian tone:
" Ah! shall we ever, ever win
  A summer of our own?"

II.

A MORN of winds and swaying trees—
    Earth's jubilance rushing out!
The birds are fighting with the breeze;
    The waters heave about.

White clouds are swept across the sky,
    Their shadows o'er the graves;
Purpling the green, they float and fly
    Athwart the sunny waves.

The long grass—an earth-rooted sea—
    Mimics the watery strife.
To boat, or horse?   Wild motion we
    Shall find harmonious life.

But whither?   Sweep and roll and bend
  Suffice for Nature's part ;
But motion to an endless end
  Is needful for our heart.

III.

THE morn awakes like brooding dove,
  With outspread wings of gray;
Her feathery clouds close in above,
  And roof a sober day.

No motion in the deeps of air !
  No trembling in the leaves !
A still contentment everywhere,
  That neither laughs nor grieves !

A film of sheeted silver gray
  Shuts in the ocean's hue ;
White-winged feluccas leave their way
  Behind in gorgeous blue.

Dream on, dream on, O dreamy day !
   Thy very clouds are dreams ·
Yon child is dreaming far away—
   He is not where he seems.

IV.

THE lark is up, his faith is strong ;
   He mounts the morning air ;
The voice of all the creature-throng,
   He sings the morning prayer.

Slow clouds from north and south appear,
   Black-based, with shining slope ;
In sullen forms their might they rear,
   And climb the vaulted cope.

A lightning flash, a thunder boom !—
   Nor sun nor clouds are there ;
A single, all-pervading gloom
   Hangs in the heavy air.

A weeping, wasting afternoon
  Weighs down the aspiring corn :
Amber and red, the sunset soon
  Leads back to golden morn.

SONGS OF THE SUMMER NIGHTS.

I.

THE dreary wind of night is out,
    Homeless and wandering slow ;
O'er pale seas moaning like a doubt,
    It breathes, but will not blow.

It sighs from out the helpless past,
    Where doleful things abide ;
Gray ghosts of dead thought sail aghast
    Across its ebbing tide.

O'er marshy pools it faints and flows,
    All deaf and dumb and blind ;
O'er moor and mountain aimless goes—
    The listless woesome wind !

Nay, nay !—breathe on, sweet wind of night !
  The sigh is all in me ;
Flow, fan, and blow, with gentle might,
  Until I wake and see.

II.

THE west is broken into bars
   Of orange, gold, and gray ;
Gone is the sun, fast come the stars,
   And night infolds the day.

My boat glides with the gliding stream,
   Following adown its breast
One flowing mirrored amber gleam,
   The death-smile of the west.

The river flows : the sky is still ;
   No ceaseless quest it knows :
Thy bosom swells, thy fair eyes fill
   At sight of such repose.

The ripples flow : unmoving sit
   The stars above the night.
In shade and gleam the waters flit :
   Yon pearly path, how bright !

III.

ALONE I lie, buried amid
  The long luxurious grass ;
The bats flit round me, born and hid
  In twilight's wavering mass.

The fir-top floats, an airy isle,
  High o'er the mossy ground ;
Harmonious silence breathes the while
  In scent instead of sound.

The flaming rose glooms swarthy red ;
  The borage gleams more blue ;
Dim-starred with white, a flowery bed
  Glimmers the rich dusk through.

Hid in the summer grass I lie,

Lost in the great blue cave ;

My body gazes at the sky,

And measures out its grave.

IV.

WHAT art thou, gathering dusky cool,
  In slow gradation fine?
Death's lovely shadow, flickering full
  Of eyes about to shine.

When weary Day goes down below,
  Thou leanest o'er his grave,
Revolving all the vanished show
  The gracious splendour gave.

Or art thou not she rather—say—
  Dark-browed, with luminous eyes,
Of whom is born the mighty Day,
  That fights and saves and dies?

For action sleeps with sleeping light ;
    Calm thought awakes with thee :
The soul is then a summer night,
    With stars that shine and see.

L.

WE bore him through the golden land,
   One early harvest morn.
The corn stood ripe on either hand—
   He knew all about the corn.

How shall the harvest gathered be
   Without him standing by ?
Without him walking on the lea,
   The sky is scarce a sky.

The year's glad work is almost done ;
   The land is rich in fruit ;
Yellow it floats in air and sun—
   Earth holds it by the root.

Why should earth hold it for a day,

   When harvest time is come ?

Death is triumphant o'er decay,

   And leads the ripened home.

II.

AND though the sun be not so warm,
  The future is not lost ;
Both corn and hope, of heart and farm,
  Lie hid from coming frost.

The sombre woods are richly sad ;
  Their leaves are red and gold :
Are thoughts in solemn splendour clad
  Signs that we men grow old ?

Strange odours haunt the doubtful brain
  From fields and days gone by ;
And mournful memories again
  Are born, are loved, and die.

The mornings clear, the evenings cool,
  Foretell no wintery wars ;
The day of dying leaves is full ;
  The night of glowing stars.

III.

'Tis late before the sun will rise;
   All early he will go;
Gray fringes hang from the gray skies,
   And wet the ground below.

Red fruit has followed golden corn;
   The leaves are few and sere;
My thoughts are old as soon as born,
   And chill with coming fear.

The winds lie sick; no softest breath
   Floats through the branches bare;
A silence as of coming death
   Is growing in the air.

But what must fade, was born to fade—
Can therefore bear the ill :
Creep on, old Winter, deathly shade !
We sorrow, and are still.

17.

THERE is no longer any heaven
　　To glorify our clouds ;
The rising vapours downward driven
　　Come home in palls and shrouds.

The sun himself is ill bested
　　A heavenly sign to show ;
His radiance, dimmed to glowing red,
　　Can hardly further go.

An earthy damp, a churchyard gloom,
　　Pervade the moveless air ;
The year is sinking in its tomb,
　　And death is everywhere.

But while sad thoughts together creep,

Like bees too cold to sting,

God's children, in their beds asleep,

Are dreaming of the spring.

SONGS OF THE AUTUMN NIGHTS.

O NIGHT, send up the harvest moon
　To walk about the fields,
And make of midnight magic noon
　On lonely tarns and wealds.

In golden ranks, with golden crowns,
　All in the yellow land,
Old solemn kings in rustling gowns,
　The sheaves moon-charmed stand.

Sky-mirror she, afloat in space,
　Beholds our coming morn:
Her heavenly joy hath such a grace,
　It ripens earthly corn;

Like some lone saint with upward eyes,

Lost in the deeps of prayer :

The people still their prayers and sighs,

And gazing ripen there.

2.

So, like the corn moon-ripened last,
   Would I, weary and gray,
On golden memories ripen fast,
   And ripening pass away.

In an old night so let me die;
   A slow wind out of doors;
A waning moon low in the sky;
   A vapour on the moors;

A fire just dying in the gloom;
   Earth haunted all with dreams;
A sound of waters in the room;
   A mirror's moony gleams;

And near me, in the sinking night,
More thoughts than move in me—
Forgiving wrong, and loving right,
And waiting till I see.

III.

ACROSS the stubble glooms the wind;
　High sails the lated crow;
The west with pallid green is lined;
　Fog tracks the river's flow.

My heart is cold and sad; I moan,
　Yet care not for my grief;
The summer fervours all are gone;
　The roses are but leaf.

Old age is coming, frosty, hoar;
　The snows of time will fall;
My jubilance, dream-like, no more
　Returns for any call.

O lapsing heart ! thy feeble strain
Sends up the blood so spare,
That my poor withering autumn brain
Sees autumn everywhere !

IV.

LORD of my life! if I am blind,
   I reck not—thou canst see;
I well may wait my summer mind,
   When I am sure of thee.

I made no brave bright suns arise,
   Veiled up no sweet gray eves;
I hung no rose-lamps, lit no eyes,
   Sent out no windy leaves.

I said not "I will cast a charm
   These gracious forms around;"
My heart with unwilled love grew warm;
   I took but what I found.

When cold winds range my winter-night,
    Be thou my summer-door;
Keep for me all my young delight,
    Till I am old no more.

SONGS OF THE WINTER DAYS.

I.

THE sky has turned its heart away,
    The earth its sorrow found;
The daisies turn from childhood's play,
    And creep into the ground.

The earth is black and cold and hard ;
    Thin films of dry white ice,
Across the rugged wheel-tracks barred,
    The children's feet entice.

Dark flows the stream as if it mourned
    The winter in the land;
With idle icicles adorned,
    That mill-wheel soon will stand.

But, friends, to say 'tis cold, and part,
Is to let in the cold ;
We'll make a summer of the heart,
And laugh at winter old.

14.

WITH vague dead gleam the morning white
  Comes through the window-panes;
The clouds have fallen all the night,
  Without the noise of rains.

Like a departing, unseen ghost,
  Footprints go from the door;
The man himself must long be lost
  Who left those footprints hoar.

Yet follow thou.   Tread down the snow.
  Leave all the road behind.
Heed not the winds that steely blow,
  Heed not the sky unkind.

G 2

For though the glittering air grow dark,
  The snow will shine till morn;
But long ere then will one fair spark
  Laugh winter all to scorn.

III.

Oh wildly wild the roaring blast
Torments the fallen snow !
The wintry storms are up at last,
And care not how they go.

In foam-like wreaths the water hoar,
Rapt whistling in the air,
Gleams through the dismal twilight frore,
A region in despair.

A spectral ocean lies outside,
Torn by a tempest dark ;
Its ghostly billows dim descried
Leap on my stranded bark.

Death-sheeted figures, long and white,

    Rave through the driving spray ;

Or, bosomed in the ghastly night,

    Shriek doom-cries far away.

IV.

A MORNING clear, with frosty light
   From sunbeams late and low ;
They shine upon the snow so white,
   And shine back from the snow.

Down tusks of ice one drop will go,
   Nor fall : at sunny noon
'Twill hang a diamond—fade, and grow
   An opal for the moon.

And when the bright sad sun is low
   Behind the mountain-dome,
A twilight wind will come and blow
   All round the children's home,

And puff and waft the powdery snow,

As feet unseen did pass.

But waiting in its bed below

Green lies the summer grass.

SONGS OF THE WINTER NIGHTS.

SEE from my window how the fire
　　Burns outside in the snow !
So love set free from love's desire
　　Lights grief of long ago.

The dark is thinned with snow-sheen fine,
　　The earth bedecked with moon ;
Out on the worlds we surely shine
　　More radiant than in June !

In the white garden lies a heap
　　As brown as deep-dug mould :
A hundred partridges that keep
　　Each other from the cold,

My father gives them sheaves of corn,
　For shelter both and food :
High hope in me was early born—
　My father was so good !

1

THE frost weaves ferns and sultry palms
 Across my clouded pane ;
Weaves melodies of ancient psalms
 All through my passive brain.

Quiet ecstasy fills heart and head :
 My father is in the room ;
The very curtains of my bed
 Are filled with sheltering gloom.

The lovely vision melts away ;
 I am a child no more ;
Work rises from the floor of play ;
 Duty is at the door.

But if I face with courage stout
  The labour and the din,
Thou, Lord, wilt let my mind go out,
  My heart with thee stay in.

III.

Up to my ear my soul doth run—
   Her other door is dark ;
There she can see without the sun,
   And there she sits to mark.

I hear the dull unheeding wind
   Rumble o'er heath and wold ;
My fancy leaves my brain behind,
   And floats into the cold.

Like a forgotten face that lies
   Among the speechless crowd,
The earth is dark, with frozen eyes,
   White-folded in her shroud.

O'er leafless woods and cornless farms,

Dead rivers, fireless thorps,

I brood, the heart still throbbing warm

In Nature's wintred corpse.

IV.

To all the world mine eyes are blind ;
  Their " drop serene " is—night,
With stores of snow piled up the wind
  An awful airy height.

And yet 'tis but a mote in the eye :
  The simple faithful stars
Beyond are shining, careless-high,
  Down on our storms and jars.

And when o'er storm and jar I climb—
  Beyond life's atmosphere,
I shall behold the lord of time
  And space—of world and year.

Oh vain far quest !—not thus my heart
　　Shall ever find its goal !
I turn me home—and there thou art,
　　My Father, in my oul !

SONGS OF THE SPRING DAYS.

1.

A GENTLE wind, of western birth
    On some far summer sea,
Wakes daisies in the wintry earth,
    Wakes hopes in wintry me.

The sun is low ; the paths are wet,
    And dance with frolic hail ;
The trees—their spring-time is not yet—
    Swing sighing in the gale.

Young gleams of sunshine peep and play ;
    Clouds shoulder in between ;
I scarce believe one coming day
    The earth will all be green.

The north wind blows, and blasts, and raves,

And flaps his snowy wing:

Back ! toss thy bergs on arctic waves ;

Thou canst not bar our spring.

4.

Up comes the primrose, wondering;
  The snowdrop drcopeth by;
The holy spirit of the spring
  Is working silently.

Soft breathing breezes woo and wile
  The later children out;
O'er woods and farms a sunny smile
  Is flickering about.

The earth was cold, hard-hearted, dull;
  To death almost she slept:
Over her heaven grew beautiful,
  And forth her beauty crept

H 2

Showers yet must fall, and waters grow

    Dark-wan with furrowing blast ;

But suns will shine, and soft winds blow,

    Till the year flowes at last.

II.

THE sky is smiling over me,
    Hath smiled away the frost;
With daisies starred the sky-like lea,
    With buds the wood embossed.

Troops of wild flowers gaze at the sky
    Up through the latticed boughs ;
Till comes the green cloud by and by,
    It is not time to house.

Yours is the day, sweet bird—sing on ;
    The winter is forgot ;
Like an ill dream, 'tis over and gone :
    Pain that is past, is not.

Joy that was past, is yet the same :

If care the summer brings,

'Twill only be another name

For love that broods, not sings.

II.

BLOW on me, wind, from west and south ;
  Sweet summer-spirit, blow !
Come like a kiss from dear child's mouth,
  Who knows not what I know.

The earth's perfection dawneth soon ;
  Ours lingereth alway ;
We have a morning, not a noon ;
  All spring, no summer gay.

Rose-blotted eve, gold-branded morn
  Crown soon the swift year's life :
In us a higher hope is born,
  And claims a longer strife.

Will heaven be an eternal spring

With summer at the door?

Or shall we one day tell its king

That we desire no more?

SONGS OF THE SPRING NIGHTS

I.

THE flush of green that dyed the day
  Hath vanished in the moon ;
The strengthened odours float and play
  An unborn, coming tune.

One southern eve like this—the dew
  Had cooled and left the ground ;
The moon hung half-way from the blue,
  No disc, but globed round :

Light-leaved acacias, by the door,
  Bathed in the balmy air ;
Clusters of blossomed moonlight bore,
  And breathed a perfume rare .·

Great gold-flakes from the starry sky

Fell flashing on the deep—

One scent of moist earth floating by

Did almost make me weep.

2

THOSE gorgeous stars were not my own ;
   They made me alien go ;
The mother o'er her head had thrown
   A veil I did not know.

The dusky fields that seaward went,
   The pale, moon-blanched glades
Bore flowering grasses, knotted, bent,
   No slender, spear-like blades.

I longed to see the starry host
   Afar in fainter blue ;
But plenteous grass I missed the most,
   With daisies glimmering through.

The common things were not the same—

    I longed across the foam :

From dew-damp earth that odour came—

    I knew the world ny home.

VI.

THE stars are glad in gulfy space—
    Friendly the dark to them !
From day's deep mine, their hiding place,
    Night wooeth every gem.

A thing for faith mid labour's jar,
    When up the day is furled,
Shines in the sky a light afar—
    Perhaps a home-filled world.

Sometimes upon the inner sky
    We catch a doubtful shine :
A mote or star ?   A flash in the eye
    Or jewel of God's mine ?

A star to us, all glimmer and glance,

May swarm with seraphim :

A fancy to our ignorance

May be a truth to him.

IV.

THE night is damp and warm and still,
    And soft with summer-dreams;
The buds are bursting at their will,
    And shy the half moon gleams.

My soul is cool, as bathed within
    By dews that silent weep—
Like child that has confessed his sin,
    And now will go to sleep.

My body ages, form and hue;
    But when the spring winds blow,
My spirit stirs and buds anew,
    Younger than long ago.

Lord, make me more a child, and more,
Till Time his own end bring ;
And out of every winter sore
I pass into thy spring.

A BOOK OF DREAMS.

VOL. III.

A BOOK OF DREAMS.

PART I.

I.

I LAY and dreamed. The master came,
　　In old wove garment drest;
Captive I stood twixt love and shame,
Not ready to be blest.

He stretched his arms, and gently sought
　　To clasp me to his heart;
I shrunk, for I, unthinking, thought
　　He knew me but in part.

I did not love him as I would ;
  Embraces were not meet ;
I dared not even stand where he stood—
  I fell and kissed his feet.

Years, years have passed away since then ;
  Oft hast thou come to me ;
The question scarce will rise again,
  Whether I care for thee.

In thee lies hid my unknown heart,
  In thee my perfect mind ;
In all my joys, my Lord, thou art
  The deeper joy behind.

But when fresh light and visions **bold**
  My heart and hope expand,
Up comes the vanity of old,
  That now I understand.

Away, away from thee I drift,
    Forgetting, not forgot ;
Till sudden yawns a downward rift—
    I start—and see thee not.

Ah, then come sad, unhopeful hours !
    All in the dark I stray,
Until my spirit fainting cowers
    On the threshold of the day.

Hence not even yet I child-like dare
    Nestle unto thy breast ;
Though well I know that only there
    Is hid the secret rest.

But now I shrink not from thy will,
    Nor guilty judge my guilt ;
Thy good shall meet and slay my ill—
    Do with me as thou wilt.

If I should dream that dream once more,
    Me in my dreaming meet ;
Embrace me, master, I implore,
    And let me kiss thy feet.

II.

1 STOOD before my childhood's home,
  Outside its belt of trees ;
All round, my glances flit and roam
  O'er well-known hills and leas ;

When sudden rushed across the plain
  A host of hurrying waves,
Loosed by some witchery of the brain,
  From far, dream-hidden caves.

And up the hill they clomb and came,
  A wild, fast flowing sea :
Careless I looked as on a game ;
  No terror woke in me.

For just the belting trees within,
  I saw my father wait ;
And should the waves the summit win,
  There was the open gate.

With him beside, all doubt was dumb ;
  There let the waters foam !
No mightiest flood would dare to come
  And drown his holy home.

Two days passed by.   With restless toss,
  The red flood brake its doors ;
Prostrate I lay, and looked across
  To the eternal shores.

'The world was fair, and hope was high;
  My friends had all been true ;
Life burned in me, and Death and I
  Would have a hard ado.

Sudden came back the dream so good,
 My trouble to abate :
At his own door my Father stood—
 I just without the gate.

" Thou know'st what is, and what appears "—
 I said ;—" mine eyes to thine
Are windows ; thou hear'st with thine ears,
 But also hear'st with mine.

" Thou know'st how me it must dismay—
 How stings the terror's goad ;
Thou art the potter—I the clay—
 'Tis thine to bear the load."

Lord, bear it ever.—Would he cry,
 My ignorant little child,
If in my arms I bore him high
 Across the moorland wild ?

I asked it not—thou madest me :

The hour, all dark behind,

Slow cometh : help me trust in thee,

For thou hast made me blind.

III.

A PIECE of gold had left my purse
  Which I had guarded ill ;
I feared a lack, but feared yet worse
  Regret returning still.

I had to lift my feeble prayer
  To him who maketh strong,
That thence no haunting thoughts of care
  Might do my spirit wrong.

And even before my body slept,
  Such visions fair I had,
That seldom soul with chamber swept
  Was more serenely glad.

No white-robed angel floated by
  On slow, reposing wings ;
I only saw, with inward eye,
  Some very common things.

First rose the scarlet pimpernel,
  With burning purple heart ;   .
I saw within it, and could spell
  The lesson of its art.

Then came the primrose, child-like flower,
  And looked me in the face ;
It bore a message full of power,
  And confidence, and grace.

And breezes rose on pastures trim,
  And bathed me all about ;
Wool-muffled sheep-bells babbled dim,
  Or only half spoke out.

Sudden swung back the door of heaven—
   But left the truth with me !
The poorest man such loss had given
   For such a gain with glee.

Thou gav'st me, Lord, a brimming cup,
   Where I bemoaned a sip ;
How easily thou didst make up
   For that my fault let slip !

What said the flowers ?   What message new
   Embalmed my soul with rest ?
I scarce can tell—only they grew
   Right out of God's own breast.

They said, God meant the flowers he made,
   Blossom and leaf and stem—
Something like what the lilies said
   When Jesus looked at them.

.

IV.

SOMETIMES, in daylight hours, awake,
  The soul with visions teems
Which to the slumbering brain would take
  The form of wondrous dreams.

In such a mood, I once descried
  A plain with steep hills bound;
A lordly company on each side
  Left bare the middle ground.

Great earthen steps at one end rise
  To something like a throne;
And thither all the radiant eyes,
  As to a centre, shone.

A snow-white glory. dim-defined,
   Those seeking eyes beseech—
Him who was not in fire or wind,
   But in the gentle speech.

They see his eyes far-fixed wait
   Adown the widening vale;
They look—but ah ! what coming fate
   Can turn such faces pale ?

It comes : in garments worn and rude,
   With faltering step and slow,
Up towards the shining multitude
   A weary man did go.

His face was white, and still-composed,
   Like one that had been dead ;
The eyes, from eyelids half unclosed.
   A faint, wan splendour shed.

His rugged crown with drops was hung,
　Like rubies dull of hue ;
His hands were pitifully wrung,
　And pierced through and through.

Silent they stood with tender awe ;
　Between the ranks he came ;
With tearful eyes they looked, and saw
　What made his feet so lame.

At length he reached the cloudy throne,
　And sank upon his knees ;
Clasped his torn hands with stifled groan,
　And spake in words like these :—

" Father, I am come back.   Thy will
　Is sometimes hard to do."
From all that multitude so still
　A sound of weeping grew.

Then mournful-glad came down the One,
　And kneeling clasped his child ;
Lay on his breast the outworn man,
　And wept until he smiled.

The people, who, in tearful woe,
　For love had almost died,
Raised aweful eyes at length—and lo !
　The two sat side by side.

V.

DREAMING I slept. Three crosses stood
  High in the gloomy air;
One bore a thief, and one the Good;
  The third cross waited bare.

A soldier coming to the place,
  Would hang me on the third;
Mine eyes they sought the master's face,
  My will the master's word.

He bent his head; I took the sign,
  And gave the error way;
Gesture nor look nor word of mine
  The secret should betray.

A moment from the cross's foot
    He turned, and left me there,
Waiting till that grim tree for fruit
    My dying form should bear.

Up rose the steaming mists of doubt,
    And chilled both heart and brain;
They shut the world of vision out,
    And fear saw only pain.

"Ah me, my hands! the hammer's blow!
    The nails that rend and pierce!
The shock may stun, but slow and slow,
    The tortúre will grow fierce.

" Alas, the awful fight with death!
    The hours to hang and die!
The thirsting gasp for common breath!
    The weakness that would cry! "

My soul returned: "A faintness soon
  Will shroud thee in its fold;
The hours will bring the fearful noon;
  'Twill pass—and thou art cold.

"'Tis his to care that thou endure,
  To curb or loose the pain;
With bleeding hands hang on thy cure—
  It shall not be in vain."

But ah! the will, which thus could quail,
  Might yield—oh, horror drear!
Then more than love, the fear to fail
  Kept down the other fear.

I stood, nor moved.   But inward strife
  The bonds of slumber broke:
Oh! had I fled, and lost the life
  Of which the master spoke?

VI.

METHINKS I hear, as o'er this life's dim dial
    The last shades darken, friends say, "*He was
        good;*"
I struggling fail to speak my faint denial—
    They whisper, "*His humility withstood.*"

I, knowing better, part with love unspoken;
    And find the unknown world not all unknown:
The bonds that held me from my centre broken,
    I seek my home, the Saviour's homely throne.

How he will greet me, walking on I wonder;
    I think I know what I will say to him:
I fear no sapphire floor of cloudless thunder,
    I fear no passing vision great and dim;

But he knows all my weary sinful story:
   How will he judge me, pure, and strong, and
      fair?
I come to him in all his conquered glory
   Won from the life that I went dreaming there!

I come; I fall before him, faintly saying:
   "Ah, Lord, shall I thy loving pardon win?
"Earth tempted me; my walk was but a straying,
   "I have no honour—but may I come in?"

I hear him say: "Strong prayer did keep me
     stable;
   "To me the earth was very lovely too:
"Thou shouldst have prayed; I would have made
     thee able
   "To love it greatly—but thou has got through."

PART II.

I.

IT is a gloomy, windy day;
  No sunny spot is bare;
Dull vapours, in uncomely play,
  Go weltering through the air:
If through the windows of my mind
  I let it come and go,
My thoughts will also in the wind
  Sweep restless to and fro.

I drop my curtains for a dream. ---
  What comes? A mighty swan,
With plumage all a sunny gleam,
  And folded airy van.

She comes, from sea-plains dreaming sent
   By sea-maids to the shore,
With stately head proud-humbly bent,
   And stroke of swarthy oar.

Lone in a vaulted rock I lie,
   A water-hollowed cell,
Where echoes of old storms go by
   Like murmurs in a shell.
The waters, half the gloomy way,
   Beneath its arches come;
Throbbing to outside billowy play,
   The green gulfs waver dumb.

Undawning twilights through the cave
   In moony glimmers go,
Half from the swan above the wave,
   Half from the swan below.

Up to my feet she gently drifts,
  Through dim, wet-shiny things;
With billowy neck thrown back, she lifts
  The shoulders of her wings.

Old earth is rich with many a nest
  Of softness ever new,
Deep, delicate, and full of rest—
  But loveliest there are two :
I may not tell them but to minds
  That are as white as they;
But none will hear, of other kinds—
  They all are turned away.

On foamy mounds betwixt the wings
  Of a white, sailing swan—
A flaky bed of shelterings—
  There you will find the one.

The other—. Well, it will not out,
  Nor need I tell it you :
I've told you one, and can you doubt,
  When there are only two ?

Fill full my dream, O splendid bird !
  Me o'er the waters bear.
Never was tranquil ocean stirred
  By ship so shapely fair !
Nor ever whiteness found a dress
  In which on earth to go,
So true, profound, and rich, unless
  It was the falling snow !

Her wings, with flutter half-aloft,
  Impatient fan her crown ;
I cannot choose but nestle soft
  Into the depth of down.

With oary-pulsing webs unseen,
    Out the white frigate sweeps;
In middle space we hang, between
    Upper and lower deeps.

Up the wave's mounting, flowing side,
    With stroke on stroke we rack;
As down the sinking slope we slide,
    She cleaves a talking track—
Like heather-bells on lonely steep,
    Like soft rain on the glass,
Like children murmuring in their sleep,
    Like winds in reedy grass.

Her white breast heaving like a wave,
    She beats the solemn time;
With slow strong sweep, intent and grave,
    She hears the ripples rhyme.

Around, from flat gloom upward drawn,
  I catch the gleam, vague, wide,
With which the wave, from dark to dawn,
  Heaves up its polished side.

The night is blue; the stars a-glow
  Crowd all the silent steep,
Pitiful o'er the restless flow
  Of the self-murmurous deep—
A thicker night, with gathered moan!
  A dull dethroned sky!
The shadows of its stars alone
  Left in to know it by!

What faints across yon lifted loop,
  Where gleams the west its last?
With sea-veiled limbs, a sleeping group
  Of Nereids dreaming past.

Row on, fair swan ;—who knows but I,
   Ere night hath sought her cave,
May see in splendour pale float by
   The Venus of the wave?

,

II.

A SPLENDOUR of dreaming o'erflowed her ;
    A glory that deepened and grew ;
A song of colour and odour
    That thrilled her through and through !
'Twas a dream of too much gladness
    Ever to see the light;
They are only dreams of sadness
    That weary out the night.

Slow darkness began to rifle
    The nest of the sunset fair;
Dank vapour began to stifle
    The scents that enriched the air.

And the flowers paled fast and faster,
  And crumbled leaf and crown,
Till they looked like the stained plaster
  Of a cornice fallen down.

And the change crept nigher and nigher,
  And inward and nearer stole,
Till the flameless but blasting fire
  Entered and withered her soul.—
But the fiend had only flouted
  Her visions of the night;
Up came the morn and routed
  The darksome things with light.

Wide awake I have often been in it—
  The dream that all is none;
It will come in the gladdest minute,
  And wither the very sun.

Two moments of sad commotion,
 One more of doubt's palsied rule –
And the great wave-pulsing ocean
 Is only a gathered pool ;

And a flower is a spot of painting,
 A lifeless, loveless hue :
Though your heart be sick to fainting,
 It says not a word to you ;
And a bird knows nothing of gladness—
 Is only a song-machine ;
A man is a reasoning madness,
 And a woman a pictured queen.

Then fiercely we dig the fountain—
 Oh ! whence do the waters rise?
Then panting we climb the mountain—
 Oh ! are there indeed blue skies ?

And we dig till the soul is weary,
    Nor find the waters out ;
And we climb till all is dreary,
    And still the sky is a doubt.

Search not the roots of the fountain,
    But drink the water bright ;
Gaze far above the mountain—
    The sky may speak in light.
But if yet thou see no beauty—
    If widowed thy heart yet cries—
With thy hands go and do thy duty,
    And thy work will clear thine eyes.

III.

A GREAT church in an empty square—
　A haunt of echoing tones ;
Feet pass not oft enough to wear
　The grass between the stones.

The jarring hinges of its gates
　A stifled thunder boom ;
The boding heart slow-listening waits,
　As for a coming doom.

The door stands wide.　With hideous grin,
　Like wicked laughter o'er,
A gulf of death, all night within,
　Hath swallowed half the floor.

Its uncouth sides of earth and clay
　　O'erhang the void below ;
Ah ! some one force my feet away,
　　Or down I needs must go.

See, see the murky, crumbling slope !
　　I would not, yet I must
Go down—for my lost loves to grope
　　Among the charnel dust.

See, see, the coffined mould glooms high !
　　Methinks, with anguish dull,
I enter by the empty eye
　　Into a monstrous skull.

Stumbling on what I dare not guess,
　　Blind wading through the gloom,
Still down, still on, I sink, I press,
　　To meet some awful doom.

My searching hands have caught a door
   With iron clenched and barred ;
Here—the gaunt spider's castle-core—
   Grim Death keeps watch and ward !

Its two leaves shake, its bars are bowed,
   As if a ghastly wind,
That never bore a leaf or cloud,
   Were pressing hard behind.

They shake, they groan, they outward strain !
   What thing of dire dismay
Will freeze its form upon my brain,
   And fright my soul away ?

They groan, they shake, they bend, they crack ;
   The bars, the doors divide :
A flood of glory at their back
   Hath burst the portals wide !—

In flows a summer afternoon ;
　I know the very breeze ;
It used to blow the silvery moon
　About the summer trees.

The gulf is filled with flashing tides ;
　Blue sky and trees look in ;
Mosses and ferns o'er floor and sides
　A mazy arras spin.

The empty church, the yawning cleft,
　The earthy, dead despair
Are gone, and I alive am left
　In sunshine and in air !

IV.

Some dreams, in slumber's twilight, sly
    Through the ivory wicket creep ;
Then suddenly the inward eye
    Sees them outside the sleep.

Once, wandering in the border gray,
    I spied one past me swim ;
I caught it on its truant way
    To nowhere in the dim.

Prone on a steep of hilly ground,
    A host of statues old !
Such forms as never more are found,
    Save deep in ancient mould !

The scattered marble Anakim
  Lay maimed, as if in fight ;
Oh, what a wealth one broken limb
  Had been to waking sight !

But sudden, the vain power to mock
  That held it to the spot,
Without a shiver or a shock,
  Behold, the dream was not !

For each dim form of marble rare,
  Bent a wind-broken reed ;
So hangs on autumn field, long bare,
  Some tall rain-battered weed.

The autumn night hung like a pall,
  Drooping above the dead ;
And if a wind had waked at all,
  It had but moaned and fled.

V.

THE simplest joys that daily pass,
Grow ecstasies in sleep ;
A wind on heights of waving grass
In dreams has made me weep.

No wonder then my heart one night
Was joy-full to the brim :
I was with one whose teaching might
Had drawn me close to him.

But from a church into the street,
Came pouring, crowding on,
A troubled throng, with hurrying feet—
And lo, my friend was gone !

Alone upon a miry road,
   I walked a wretched plain ;
Onward without a goal I strode,
   Through mist and drizzling rain.

Low mounds of ruin, ugly pits,
   And brick-fields scarred the globe ;
Those wastes where desolation sits
   Without her ancient robe.

The dreariness, the nothingness
   Grew worse almost than fear ,
If ever hope was needful bliss,
   Hope sure was needful here !

Was my wish father to the change,
   In some dream-bearing cell ?
Wishes not always fruitless range,
   And sometimes it is well.

I know not.   Sudden sank the way !
Burst in the ocean-waves !
Behold a bright blue-billowed bay,
Red rocks and sounding caves !

Dreaming I wept.   Awake, I ask—
Shall Earth in dreams uncouth
Set the old Heavens too hard a task
To match them with the truth ?

VI.

ONCE more I build a dream, awake,
  Which sleeping I would dream ;
Once more an unborn fancy take,
  And try to make it seem.
Some strange delight shall fill my breast,
  Enticed from sleep's abyss,
With sense of motion yet of rest,
  Of sleep, yet waking bliss.

It comes ! I lie on something warm,
  That lifts me from below ;
It holds me like a mighty arm,
  Though soft as drifted snow.

A dream, indeed !—Oh, happy me
  Whom Titan woman bears
Afloat upon a gentle sea
  Of wandering midnight airs !

A breeze, just cool enough to lave
  With sense each conscious limb,
Glides round and under, like a wave
  Of twilight growing dim !
She bears me over sleeping towns,
  O'er murmuring ears of corn ;
O'er tops of trees, o'er billowy downs,
  O'er moorland wastes forlorn.

The harebells in the mountain-pass
  Flutter their blue about ;
The myriad blades of meadow grass
  Float scarce-heard music out.

A BOOK OF DREAMS.

Over the lake!—ah ! nearer float,
    'Nearer the water's breast ;
Let me look deeper—let me doat
    Upon that lily-nest.

Old homes we brush—in wood, on road ;
    Their windows do not shine ;
Their dwellers must be all abroad
    In lovely dreams like mine.
Hark ! drifting syllables that break
    Like foam-bells on fleet ships !
The little airs are all awake
    With softly kissing lips.

Light laughter ripples down the wind,
    Sweet sighs float everywhere ;
But when I look I nothing find,
    For every star is there.

O lady lovely, lady strong,
　　Ungiven thy best gift lies !
Why bear me in thine arms along,
　　Yet not reveal thine eyes ?

Pale doubt lifts up a snaky crest ;
　　In darts a pang of loss ;
My outstretched hand, for hills of rest,
　　Finds only heaps of moss.
Beneath faint stars I sit in fear ;
　　The wind begins to weep :
'Tis night indeed, chilly and drear,
　　And all but me asleep.

ROADSIDE POEMS.

ROADSIDE POEMS.

BETTER THINGS.

BETTER to smell the violet cool
Than sip the glowing wine ;
Better to hark a hidden brook,
Than watch a diamond shine.

Better the love of gentle heart,
Than beauty's favours proud ;
Better the rose's living seed,
Than roses in a crowd.

Better to love in loneliness,
Than bask in love all day;
Better the fountain in the heart,
Than the fountain by the way.

Better be fed by mother's hand,
Than eat alone at will;
Better to trust in God, than say,
My goods my storehouse fill.

Better to be a little wise,
Than in knowledge to abound;
Better to teach a child, than toil
To fill perfection's round.

Better sit at a master's feet,
Than thrill a listening state;
Better suspect that thou art proud,
Than be sure that thou art great.

Better to walk the realm unseen,
Than watch the hour's event ;
Better the *well-done* at the last,
Than the air with shoutings rent.

Better to have a quiet grief,
Than a hurrying delight ;
Better the twilight of the dawn,
Than the noonday burning bright.

Better a death when work is done,
Than earth's most favoured birth ;
Better a child in God's great house,
Than the king of all the earth.

AN OLD SERMON WITH A NEW TEXT.

My wife contrived a fleecy thing
    Her husband to infold,
For 'tis the pride of woman still,
    To cover from the cold :
My daughter made it a new text
    For a sermon very old.

The child came trotting to her side,
    Ready with bootless aid :
" Lily will make one for papa,"
    The tiny woman said :
Her mother gave the needful things,
    With a knot upon the thread.

" The knot, mamma !—it won't come through.

    Mamma ! mamma ! " she cried.

Her mother cut away the knot,

    And she was satisfied,

Pulling the long thread through and through,

    In fabricating pride.

Her mother told me this : I caught

    A glimpse of something more :

Great meanings often hide themselves

    With little words before ;

And I brooded over the new text,

    Till the seed a sermon bore.

Nannie, to you I preach it now—

    A little sermon, low :

Is it not thus a thousand times,

    As through the world we go,

When we keep tugging, fretting—crying,
　　Instead of " Yes, Lord," " No " ?

For all the rough things that we meet,
　　Which will not move a jot—
The hindrances to heart and feet—
　　The Crook in every Lot—
What mean they, but that children's threads
　　Have at the end a knot ?

For *circumstance* is God's great web—
　　He gives it free of cost,
But we must make it into clothes
　　To shield our hearts from frost :
Shall we, because the thread holds fast,
　　Count all our labour lost ?

If he should cut away the knot,
　　And yield each fancy wild,

The hidden life within our hearts—
   His life, the undefiled—
Would fare as ill as I should fare
   From the needle of my child.

For as the cordage to the sail ;
   As to my verse the rhyme ;
As mountains to the low green earth—
   So fair, so hard to climb ;
As call of striking clock, amid
   The quiet flow of time ;

As sculptor's mallet to the birth
   Of the slow-dawning face ;
As knot upon my Lily's thread,
   When she would work apace ;
God's *Nay* is such, and worketh so
   For his children's coming grace.

Who knowing his ideal end,
   Such birthright would refuse?
What makes us what we have to be
   Is the only thing to choose :
We neither know his end nor means,
   And yet his will accuse !

This is my sermon.   It is preached
   Against all fretful strife.
Chafe not with anything that is,
   Nor cut it with thy knife.
Ah ! be not angry with the knot
   That holdeth fast thy life.

LITTLE ELFIE.

I HAVE a puppet-jointed child,
   Only three half-years old ;
Through lawless hair her eyes gleam wild.
   With looks both shy and bold.

Like little imps, her tiny hands
   Dart out and push and take ;
Chide her—a trembling thing she stands,
   And like two leaves they shake.

But to her mind, a minute gone
   Is like a year ago ;
And when you lift your eyes anon,
   Anon you must say *no*.

Sometimes, though not oppressed with care,
 She has her sleepless fits ;
Then, blanket-swathed, in that round chair
 The elfish mortal sits ;—

Where, if by chance in mood more grave,
 A hermit she appears,
Propped in the opening of his cave,
 Mummied almost with years.

Or like an idol set upright
 With folded legs for stem,
Ready to hear prayers all the night,
 And never answer them.

But where's the idol-hermit thrust ?
 Like flails her knee-joints go—
Now this, now that !—her mother must
 Alternate kiss each toe.

But if I turn away and write
    For minutes three or four—
A tiny spectre, tall and white,
    She's standing by the door—

Long-robed—like stately Mrs. Ham,
    Entering her Noah's-ark :
She'd change the lion to a lamb
    By shining through the dark !

Again a thought comes in my head,
    And I must sit and think ;—
She's on the table, the quadruped!
    And dabbling in my ink !

O Elfie, make no haste to lose
    Thy lack of grown-up sense ;
Thou hast the best gift I could choose—
    A fearless confidence.

THE SHADOWS.

My little boy, with smooth fair cheeks,
  And dreamy, large, brown eyes,
Not often, little wisehead, speaks,
  But what he hears, he tries.

" God is not only in the sky"—
  His sister said one day;
For she was sometimes pleased to cry
  Like Wisdom in the way:

"He's in this room."   Dreamy yet clear,
  His eyes went round for God.
Vain all to look, vain all to peer !—
  His wits are quite abroad.

" He is not here, mamma ?   No, no ;
    I do not see him at all.
He's not the shadows. is he ? "   So
    His doubtful accents fall—

Fall on my heart—no babble mere !
    They rouse both love and shame :
But for the loneliness and fear,
    I still had thought the same.

Ah ! sometimes, ere the morning break,
    And home the shadows flee,
In my dim room even yet I take
    The shadows, Lord, for thee !

THE CHILD-MOTHER.

HEAVILY slumbered noonday-light
Upon the lone field—shining bright,
   A burnished grassy sea :
The child, in cloudless golden hours,
Through nebulae of sunny flowers,
   Went walking on the lea.

Velvety bees make busy hum ;
Green flies and striped wasps go and come ;
   The butterflies are white ;
Blue-burning, vaporous, to and fro,
The dragon-flies like arrows go,
   Or hang in moveless flight.

Nothing she followed; like a rill,

She wandered on with quiet will;

   Received, but did not miss;

Her step was neither quick nor long;

And sometimes a half-murmured song

   Breathed her half-conscious bliss.

The little spirit-stately child

Was never frolicsome and wild

   As such a girl might be—

But now, though nine and nothing more,

Another little child she bore,

   Almost as big as she.

No silken cloud from solar harms

Had she to spread—with straining arms

   She turned him from the sun;

Mother and sister both in heart,

She did a gracious woman's part.
  Her lovely task begun.

And now they gain a stagnant ditch,
The slippery sloping banks of which
  More varied blossoms line ;
Some ragged-robins baby spies,
And spreads his arms, and crows and cries—
  Which means " They must be mine."

What baby wants, that baby has—
A law unalterable as—
  The poor shall serve the rich :
Had baby only been a post !
But, overreaching, too engrossed,
  She topples in the ditch.

Adown the slope she slanting rolled ;
But her two arms convulsive hold

The precious baby tight;
She lets herself sublimely go,
Till in the ditch's muddy flow
    She stands—in evil plight.

Her stockings soiled she might forget,
But her new shoes !—they're soaking wet !
    And still she does not cry ;
For though her frock and tippet blue
And petticoat are all wet through,
    The baby is quite dry !

And baby laughs, and baby crows ;
And baby being right, she knows
    That nothing can be wrong
So with a troubled heart, yet stout
She plans how *ever* to get out,
    With meditation long.

The high bank's edge is far away,
The slope is steep, and crossing clay ;
   And what to do with baby ?
For even a monkey, up to run,
Would need his four hands, every one :—
   She is perplexed as may be.

But all her puzzling was no good ;
Blank staring up the side she stood,
   Which, as she sunk, grew higher ;
Till a fresh inroad of dismay,
Lest baby's patience should give way,
   Plucked her feet from the mire.

And up and down the ditch, not glad,
But patient, she did promenade—
   Splash went her little feet !
And baby thought it rare good fun,

With added help of one half-bun,
    And endless meadow-sweet.

But, oh, the world that she had left !
The meads from her so lately reft—
    An infant Proserpine !
A fabled land they lay above,
A paradise of sunny love, .
    In breezy room divine !

And often from the village green,
Came sounds of laughter, faintly keen,
    And bark of well-known dogs ;
While she, the hot sun overhead,
Her lonely watery way must tread,
    In mud and weeds and frogs.

Sudden, the ditch about her shakes ;
Her little heart, responsive, quakes

With fear of uncouth woes;
She lifts her boding eyes perforce,
And sees the huge head of a horse
    Go past upon its nose.

Then hark! what sounds of tearing grass
And puffing breath!—With knobs of brass
    On horns of frightful size,
A cow's head through the broken hedge
Looks awful from the other edge,
    Though mild her pondering eyes.

The horse, the cow are passed and gone;
The sun keeps going on and on;
    And still no help comes near.
At misery's last—oh joy! the sound
Of human footsteps on the ground!
    She almost shrieked "*I'm* here!"

It was a man—oh, heavenly joy !
He looked amazed at girl and boy,
   And reached his hand so strong :
" Give me the child," he said ; but no !
Love could not let the burden go
   Which it had borne so long.

With well-pleased laugh at her alarms,
He kneeled, and brought her—babe in arms—
   Back to the world again.
Her low thanks feebly murmured, she
Dragged her legs homeward painfully—
   Poor, wet, one-chickened hen !

At home at length—lo, scarce a speck
Was on the child from heel to neck,
   Though she was sorely mired !
No tear confessed the long-drawn rack,

Till, having given the baby back,
   She cried, "Oh me ! I'm tired."

Then, intermixed with sobbing wail,
She told her mother all the tale—
   On her wet cheeks a glow :
" But, mother, even when I fell,
I kept the baby pretty well—
   1 never let him go."

HE HEEDED NOT.

Of whispering trees the tongues to hear,
   And sermons of the silent stone;
To read in brooks the print so clear
   Of motion, shadowy light, and tone—
That man hath neither eye nor ear
   Who careth not for human moan.

Yea, he who draws, in shrinking haste,
   From sin that passeth helpless by;
The weak antennæ of whose taste
   From touch of alien grossness fly—
Shall, banished to the outer waste,
   Never in Nature's bosom lie.

But he whose heart is full of grace
    To his own kindred all about,
Shall find in lowest human face,
    Blasted with wrong and dull with doubt,
More than in Nature's holiest place
    Where mountains dwell and streams run out.

Coarse cries of strife assailed mine ear,
    In suburb-ways, one summer morn ;
A wretched alley I drew near—
    Sad place where such might well be born—
Growls breaking into curses clear,
    And shrill retort of keener scorn.

Slow from its narrow entrance came—
    His senses drowned with revels dire—
Scarce fit to answer to his name—
    A man consumed in smouldering ire :

HE HEEDED NOT.

Flashes of sullen, fitful flame
    Broke from the embers of his fire.

He cast a glance of stupid hate
    Behind him, every step he took ;
Where followed him, like following fate,
    An aged crone, with bloated look ;
A something checked his listless gait—
    She neared him, rating till she shook.

What kept him—thus to be disgraced?
    A love—too thoughtful to be coy :
In front, no higher than his waist,
    Half-buttressed him a tiny boy—
An earnest child, ill-clothed, pale-faced,
    Whose eyes held neither hope nor joy.

Perhaps you think he pushed, and pled
    With parent wroth—to keep the peace

And home his footsteps would have led,
 To find in sleep his sin's release ;—
Poor children know the good of bed,
 To make the drunken fever cease.

No; though like unfledged, hungry bird,
 He stood on tiptoe, reaching higher,
To one expostulating word
 His anxious soul did not aspire ;
With humbler care his heart was stirred,
 With humbler service to his sire.

With waking pale, with anger red,
 He, forward leaning, held his foot
Lest on the darling he should tread :
 A misty sense had taken root
Somewhere in his bewildered head,
 That round him kindness hovered mute.

Harmless his words as babbling rill
  Passed o'er the child's head zephyr-borne ;
Unscathed as bee whose dodging skill
  And myriad eyes the hail-shower scorn,
He, following his eager will,
  Buttoned his father's waistcoat worn.

Over his calm, unconscious face,
  No motion passed, no change of mood ;
Still as a pool in its own place,
  Unsunned within an umbrose wood.
It kept its quiet shadowy grace,
  As round it all things had been good.

Was the boy deaf—the tender palm
  Of him that made him, folded round
The little head, to keep it calm
  With a *hitherto* to every sound—

And so nor curse nor shout nor psalm
   Could thrill the globe thus grandly bound ?

Or came in force the happy law,
   That customed things themselves erase ?
Or was he too intent for awe ?
   Did lové take all the thinking place ?
I cannot tell ; I only saw
   An earnest, fearless, hopeless face.

THE SHEEP AND THE GOAT.

THE thousand streets of London gray
   Repel all country sights ;
But bar not winds upon their way,
Nor quench the scent of new-mown hay
   In depth of summer nights.

And here and there an open spot,
   Still bare to light and dark,
With grass receives the wanderer hot :
There trees are growing, houses not—
   They call the place a park.

Soft creatures, with ungentle guides,
   God's sheep from hill and plain,

Flow thitherward in fitful tides,

There weary lie on woolly sides,

   Or crop the grass amain.

And from dark alley, yard, and den,

   In ragged skirts and coats,

Troop hither tiny sons of men,

Wild things, untaught of word or pen—

   The little human goats.

In Regent's Park one cloudless day,

   An overdriven sheep,

Arrived from long and dusty way,

Throbbing with thirst and hotness lay,

   A panting woollen heap.

But help is nearer than we know

   For ills of every name :

Ragged enough to scare the crow,

But with a heart to pity woe,

    A quick-eyed urchin came.

Little he knew of field or fold,

    Yet knew what ailed; his cap

Was ready cup for water cold;

Though rumpled, stained, and very old,

    Its rents were small—good-hap!

Shaping the rim and crown he went,

    Till crown from rim was deep.

The water gushed from pore and rent;

Before he came one half was spent—

    The other saved the sheep.

O little goat, born, bred in ill,

    Unwashed, half-fed, unshorn!

Thou to the sheep from breezy hill
Wast bishop, pastor, what you will,
  In London dry and lorn.

And let priests say the thing they please,
  My hope, though very dim,
Thinks he will say who always sees,
In doing it to one of these
  Thou didst it unto him.

THE WAKEFUL SLEEPER.

WHEN things are holding wonted pace
In wonted paths, without a trace
   Or hint of neighbouring wonder,
Sometimes, from other realms, a tone,
A scent, a vision, swift, alone,
   Breaks common life asunder.

Howe'er it comes, whate'er its door,
It makes you ponder something more—
   Unseen with seen things linking :
To neighbours met one festive night,
Was given a quaint and lovely sight,
   That set some of them thinking.

They stand, in music's fetters bound,
By a clear brook of warbled sound—
    A canzonet of Haydn—
When the door slowly comes ajar—
A little further—just as far
    As show a tiny maiden.

Softly she enters, her pink toes
Daintily peeping, as she goes,
    Her long nightgown from under.
The varied mien, the questioning look
Were worth a picture; but she took
    No notice of their wonder.

They made a path, and she went through :
She had her little chair in view,
    Close by the chimney-corner.
She turned—sat down before them all,

Stately as princess at a ball,
  And silent as a mourner.

Then looking closer yet, they spy
What mazedness hid from every eye,
  As ghost-like she came creeping :
They see that though sweet little Rose
Her settled way unerring goes,
  The child is plainly sleeping.

" Play on, sing on," the mother said ;
" Oft music draws her from her bed."—
  Dumb Echo, she sat listening.
Over her face the sweet concent
Like winds o'er placid waters went ;
  Her cheeks like eyes were glistening.

Her hands tight-clasped her bent knees hold ·
Like long grass drooping on the wold,

Her sightless head is bending ,
She sits all ears, and drinks her fill ;
Then rising goes, sedate and still,
On silent white feet wending.

Surely, while she was listening on,
Fine things must to her heart have gone—
Comfort 'gainst coming sorrow ;
Sweet hope to help her in the day
When earnest creeps into her play,
Which must be some to-morrow.

And little as she then will know
Whence come the hopes to meet the woe—
From what far fields they gather,
As little know we what, when sleep
Is bathing us in stillness deep,
Comes to us from the Father.

A DREAM OF WAKING.

A CHILD was born in sin and shame,
   Wronged by his very birth,
Without a home, without a name,
   One over in the earth.

No wifely triumph he inspired,
   Allayed no husband's fear;
Intruder bare, whom none desired,
   He had a welcome drear.

Heaven's beggar, all but turned adrift
   For knocking at earth's gate,
His mother him, like evil gift,
   Shunned with a sickly hate.

And now the mistress on her knee
    The unloved baby bore,
The while the servant sullenly
    Prepared to leave her door.

Her eggs are dear to mother-dove,
    Her chickens to the hen ;
All young ones bring with them their love—
    Of sheep, or goats, or men ;

This one lone child shall not have come
    In vain for love to seek :
Let mother's hardened heart be dumb,
    A sister-babe will speak.

"Mother, keep baby—keep him *so.*
    Don't let him go away."
"But, darling, if his mother go,
    Poor baby cannot stay."

" He's crying, mother : don't you see
    He wants to stay with you ? "
" No, child; he does not care for me."
    " Do keep him, mother—*do*."

" For his own mother he would cry—
    He's hungry now, I think."
" Give him to me, and let *me* try
    If I can make him drink.

"Susan would hurt him. Mother *will*
    Let the poor baby stay ?"
The mother-heart grew sore—but still
    Baby must go away.

The red lip trembled; the slow tears
    Came darkening in her eyes ;
Pressed on her heart a weight of fears
    That found no ease in cries.

'Twas torture—must not be endured—
A too outrageous grief!
Was there an ill could *not* be cured?
She *would* find some relief.

All round her universe she pried;
No dawn began to break :
In prophet-agony she cried—
"Mother! when *shall* we wake?"

O insight born of torture's might !—
Such grief *can* only seem.
Rise o'er the hills, eternal light,
And melt the earthly dream.

A MANCHESTER POEM.

'TIS a poor drizzly morning, dark and sad.
The cloud has fallen, and filled with fold on fold
The chimneyed city; and the smoke is caught,
And spreads diluted in the cloud, and sinks,
A black precipitate, on miry streets;
And faces gray glide through the darkened fog.

Slave engines lift once more their ugly growl.
The bands of iron and blocks of squared stone,
That cage them to their task, strain, quivering, till
The city trembles; and the clamour of bells,
Importunate, keeps calling pale-faced forms

To come and feed those engines' groaning strength
With fire and labour. See amongst them two,
Much like the rest—the woman with her gown
Drawn over her head—the man with bended neck
Submissive to the rain : amid the jar,
And clash, and shudder of the awful force,
They enter and part—each to a different task,
But each a soul of knowledge to brute force,
Working a will through the organized whole
Of cranks, and belts, and levers, pinions, and
      screws,
Wherewith small man has eked his body out.

And labouring thus, they pass the murky day,
In floating dust of swift revolving wheels,
And filmy spoil of quick contorted threads,
Which weave a sultry chaos all about;
Until, at length, old darkness, swelling slow
Up from the caves of night to make an end,

Chokes in its tide the clanking of the looms,

The monster-engines, and the flying gear ;

Earth draws her curtains, and sits down to nurse

Her children—as a mother-ghost may sit

With her neglected darlings in the dark ;

And home they walk, with sense of glad release.

   Home—to a dreary place !   Unfinished walls,

Earth-heaps, and broken bricks, and muddy

      pools,

Lie round it like a rampart against the spring,

The summer, and all changing of the year.

But lo ! when darkness opens an eye of fire,

The room reveals a temple, proven by signs

Seen in the ancient place.   For here is light,

Yea burning fire, with darkness on its skirts;

Bread; and pure water, ready to baptize;

And in the twilight edges of the light,

A book; and, for the cunning-woven veil,

Their faces—hiding God's own place behind ;
Even their bed figures the would-be grave
Where One arose triumphant, slept no more ;
And at an altar-table they sit down
To eat their Eucharist—for to the heart
Of him who reads the will in the command,
Love is made flesh as often as he eats.

A while with silence resting—spirit-sleep,
They gradually grow aware of light
That overcomes their light, and, through the blind,
Casts from the window-frame two shadow-glooms
That make a cross of darkness on the white.
The woman rises, eagerly she looks ;
And lo, a wind has mown the earth-sprung fog.
And far aloft, the white exultant moon,
From her blue window, curtained all with white,
Sends greetings to their window, dingy, low.
Smiling she turns ; he understands the smile :

To-morrow will be fair—as holy, fair !
Then lying down, in sleep they die till morn ;
And through their night throb low aurora-gleams
Of resurrection and the coming dawn.

They wake : 'tis Sunday. Still the moon is there,
But thin and ghostly—clothed upon with light,
As if, while they were sleeping, she had died.
They dress themselves, like priests, in clean attire,
And, through their lowly door, enter God's room.

One side the street, the windows all are moons
To light the others that in shadow lie.
See down the sun-side an old woman come
In a red cloak that makes the whole street glad !
A long-belated autumn-flower she seems,
Dazed by the rushing of the new-born life
Up hidden stairs to see the calling sun ;
But in her cloak and smile—there speaks the spring.

Through slow dissolving streets, towards glim-
    mers of green,
They pass—oh, far the streets repel the spring!
Yet every stone in the beaten pavement shares
The life that thrills anew the outworn earth—
A right Bethesda angel—for all, not some!
A street unfinished leads them forth at length
Where green fields bask, and hedgerow trees apart
Stand waiting in the air as for some good,
And the sky is broad and blue—and there is all!
No peaceful river meditates along
The weary flat to the less level sea!
No forest brown, on pillared stems, and boughs
Bent in great gothic arches, bears aloft
A groined vault, fretted with tremulous leaves!
No mountains lift their snows, and send their brooks
Down babbling with the news of silent things!
But love itself is commonest, loveliest;
The sacrifice lieth at every door;

And he that hath not forest, brook, or hill,
Must learn to read aright what commoner books
Unfold before him.   If ocean solitudes—
Then darkness dashed with glory, infinite shades,
And misty minglings of the sea and sky.
If only fields—the humble man of heart
Will revel in the grass beneath his foot,
And from the lea lift his glad eye to heaven—
God's palette, where his careless artist hand
Sweeps comet-clouds, that net the gazing soul ;
Streaks endless stairs, and blots half-sculptured
     blocks ;
Curves filmy pallours ; heaps huge mountain-
     crags ;
Nor touches where it leaves not beauty's mark.

  To them the sun and air are feast enough,
As through field-paths and lanes they slowly walk;
But sometimes, on the far horizon dim

A veil is lifted, and they spy the hills,

Cloudlike and faint, yet sharp against the sky ;

Then wakes an unknown want, which asks and
    looks

As for some thing forgot—loved long ago,

But on the hither verge of childhood dropt :

Home-sickness of the soul, roused by the spring !

For fresh birth, eager growth, reviving life,

Which *is* because it *would be*, fill the world.

The very light is new-born with the grass :

The stones themselves are warm ; the brown
    earth swells,

Filled, sponge-like, with dark beams, which nestle
    close,

And brood unseen, and sly, and potent warm,

In every little corner, nest, and crack,

Where buried lurks a blind and sleepy seed,

Waiting the touch of the finger of the sun.

The mossy stems and boughs, where yet no life

Oozes exuberant in brown and green,

Are clad in golden splendours, crossed and lined

With shuttle-shadows weaving lovely change.

Through the tree-tops the west wind rushing goes,

Calling and rousing the dull sap within :

The fine jar down the stem sinks tremulous,

From airy root thrilling to earthy branch.

And though as yet no buddy dots of light

Sparkle the darkness of the hedgerow twigs,

The smoke-dried bark appears to spread and
       swell

In the soft nurture of the warm light-bath.

   The early sun has crossed the key-stone height

Of his low arch : **they** turn them strengthened
      home ;—

Filled with pure air, and light, **and** operant spring,

They, like the bees, go back to their dark house

To store their innocent spoil—in honeyed thought.

But on their way, crossing a field, they chance
Upon a spot where there had been a home ;
Low roots of walls peer up, o'ergrown with moss—
A small dead cottage, all but mouldered quite ;
A vanished human care still shadows it ;
The little garden's half out-blotted map
Is yet discernible because the grass
Is thinner on the walks.   There, in the midst
Of bushes dry, dead flowers, uncomely weeds,
A single snowdrop droops its snowy drop—
The lonely remnant of a family
That in the garden dwelt about the home,
Reviving with the spring—and none to see !

They see, and its ideal counterpart
Awakes and blossoms white in their meek souls—
A longing, patient, waiting-hopefulness,
The first-born of the heart!   A heavenly child
Pale with the earthly cold, it hangs its head :

But they in whom it dwells enduringly,
Inherit in their meekness all the world.

I love thee, flower, with an almost human
    love.
Lo, on thine inner leaves and in thy heart
The loveliest green, acknowledging the grass—
White-minded memory of lowly friends !
But almost more I love thee for the earth
Which clings to thy transfigured radiancy,
Uplifted with thee from thine abandoned grave ;
Say rather the soiling of thy garments pure
Upon thy road into the light and air,
The heaven of thy new birth. Some gentle rain
Will one day wash thee white, and send the
    earth
Back to the earth ; but, sweet friend, while it
    clings,
I love the cognizance of our family.

With careful hands uprooting it, they bear
The little plant a willing captive home—
Fearless of dark abode, because secure
In its own tale of light.   As once of old
When the angel of the annunciation shone,
It bears all heaven into a common house.
A pot of mould its one poor tie to earth,
Its heaven an ell of blue 'twixt chimney-tops,
Its world the priests of that small temple-room,
It takes its prophet-place with fire and book,
Type of primeval spring, whose mighty arc
Hath not yet drawn the summer up our sky.
At night, when the dark shadow of the cross
Will enter, clothed in moonlight, still and wan,
Like a pale mourner at its foot, the flower
Will drooping wait the dawn.   Then the dark bird
With jewelled breast, which hangs wire-caged
      above,
Will break into its prisoned-angel song.

Weary and hopeful, to their sleep they go;
And all night long the snowdrop glimmers white
Amid the dark, unconscious and unseen.

Out of my verse I woke, and saw my room,
My precious books, the cherub-forms above;
And rose, and walked abroad, and sought the
    woods.
And roving odours met me on my way.

I entered Nature's church, a shimmering vault
Of boughs, and clouded leaves—filmy and pale
Betwixt me and the sun; low at my feet
Their shadows looked more solid than them-
    selves,
And lay like tombstones o'er the vanished flowers.
Silent the place, except for broken songs
Of some Memnonian, glory-stricken birds
That burst into a carol and were still;

And moveless but that golden beetles crept,
Green goblins, in the roots; and squirrel things
Ran, wild as cherubs, through the tracery ;
And here and yonder a flaky butterfly
Was doubting in the air, scarlet and blue.

But 'twixt my heart and summer's perfect grace,
Drove a dividing wedge;—and far away
It seemed, like voice heard loud yet far away
By one who, waking half, soon sleeps outright.
—Where was the snowdrop? where the flower of
        hope?
In me the spring was throbbing—and around
I saw the resting, odour-breathing summer !
My heart heaved swelling like a prisoned bud,
And summer crushed it with its weight of light.

Winter is full of stings and sharp reproofs,
Lovely and needful, but like cold sister's words ;

And summer is too complete for growing hearts ;

Too idle its noons, too arrowy its morns,

Too full of slumberous dreams its dusky eves.

We need a broken season, and a land

Whose shadows ever point from here away ;

A scheme of cones abrupt, and shattered spheres,

And circles cut to widen evermore.

To us, a flower of winter-harassed spring,

Crocus, or primrose, or anemone,

Is lovely as was never rosiest rose ;

A heath-bell on a waste lonely and dry

Says more than lily stately in breathing white ;

A window fair through vaulted roof of rain,

Lets in a light that comes from farther away,

And, sinking deeper, spreads a finer joy,

Than cloudless noon-tide splendorous o'er the
world.

Man seeks a better home than Paradise ;

Therefore high hope is more than deepest joy ;

The first meek daisy on a wind-swept lea,
Dearer than Eden-groves with rivers four.

Yet if my heart were pure, perhaps the rose
Were but the primrose of a higher spring ;
The sun-flower but a daisy of the prime
That leads high summer in for full-blown hearts.

POEMS FOR CHILDREN.

POEMS FOR CHILDREN.

LESSONS FOR A CHILD.

I.

THERE breathes not a breath of the
summer air,
But the spirit of love is moving there ;
Not a trembling leaf on the shadowy tree,
Flutters with hundreds in harmony,
But the spirit can part its tone from the rest,
And read the life in its beetle's breast.
When the sunshiny butterflies come and go,
Like flowers paying visits to and fro,
Not a single wave of their fanning wings
Is unfelt by the spirit that feeleth all things.

The long-mantled moths, that sleep at noon,

And rove in the light of the gentler moon ;

And the myriad gnats that dance like a wall,

Or a moving column that will not fall ;

And the dragon-flies that go burning by,

Shot like a glance from a seeking eye—

All have one being that loves them all :

Not a fly in a spider's web can fall,

But he cares for the spider, and cares for the fly.

He cares much whether you laugh or cry;

More whether your mother smile or sigh.

How it can be, I do not know ;

But it would be strange if it were not so—

Dreadful and dreary for even a fly ;

So I cannot wait for the *how* and *why*,

But believe that all things are gathered and nursed

In the love of him whose love went first,

And made this world—like a huge great nest

For a hen to sit on with feathery breast,

II.

THE bird on the leafy tree,
The bird in the cloudy sky,
The hart in the forest free,
The stag on the mountain high,
The fish inside the sea,
The albatross asleep
On the outside of the deep,
The bee through the summer sunny
Hunting for wells of honey—
What is the thought in the breast
.Of the little bird in its nest?
What is the thought in the songs
The lark in the sky prolongs?
What mean the dolphin's rays,
Winding his watery ways?

What is the thought of the stag,

Stately on yonder crag?

What does the albatross think,

Dreaming upon the brink

Of the mountain billow, and then

Dreaming down in its glen?

What is the thought of the bee

Fleeting so silently,

Or flitting—with busy hum,

But a careless go-and-come—

From flower-chalice to chalice,

Like a prince from palace to palace?

What makes those almost merry?

What makes them alive—so very?

And these so stately calm,

They might be singing a psalm?

I do not know what they think;

But gladly they eat and drink.

And on all that lies about,

- With a quiet heart look out,

After their kind, stately or coy,

Solemn like man, gamesome like boy,

Each with its own mysterious joy.

And God who knows their thoughts and ways,

Though his the creatures do not know,

From his fills every heart of theirs ;

Over them all his breath doth blow ;

His own good things with them he shares,

Is content with their bliss, and wants no prayers,

But takes their joy for praise.

If thou wouldst be like him, go

And be kind with a kindness undefiled ;

For they who give for thanks, my child,

His joy shall never know.

III.

Root met root in the spongy ground,
    Searching about for food :
Each the other went half around,
    And each got something good.

Sound met sound in the wavy air—
    That made a little to-do :
They jostled not long, but were quick and fair;
    Each found its path and flew.

Drop dashed on drop, as the rain-shower fell:
    They joined and sunk below.
In gathered thousands they rose a well,
    With a singing overflow.

Wind met wind in a garden green ;
   Both began to fret :
A tearing whirlwind arose between—
   There love lies bleeding yet.

WHAT MAKES SUMMER?

WINTER froze the brook and well ;
Fast and fast the snow-flakes fell :
Children gathered round the hearth,
Made a summer of their mirth.
One—a child so lately come
That his life was yet one sum
Of delights—all games and rambles,
Nights of dreams, and days of gambols—
Thought aloud : "I wish I knew
What makes summer—that I do : "
And the answer to his question
Held the truth, half in suggestion.
   'Tis the sun that rises early,

WHAT MAKES SUMMER?

Shining, shining all day rarely;

Drawing up the larks to meet him,

Earth's bird-angels, wild to greet him;

Drawing up the clouds, to pour

Down again a shining shower;

Drawing out the grass and clover—

Blossoms breaking out all over;

Drawing out the flowers to stare

At their father in the air—

He all light, they how much duller!

Yet son-suns of every colour;

Drawing out the flying things—

Out of eggs, fast-flapping wings;

Out of lumps like frozen snails,

Butterflies with splendid sails;

Drawing buds from all the trees;

From their hives the buzzy bees;

Living gold from earthy cracks—

Beetles with their burnished backs;

Drawing laughter out of water,
Smiling small suns as he taught her;
Sending winds to every nook,
That no creature be forsook;
Drawing children out of doors,
On two legs, or on all fours;
Drawing out of gloom and sadness,
Hope and blessing, peace and gladness;
Making man's heart sing and shine
With his brilliancy divine.

Slow at length, adown the west,
Lingering, he goes to rest;
Like a child, who, blissful yet,
Is unwilling to forget,
And, though sleepy, heels and head,
Thinks he cannot go to bed.
Even when down behind the hill,
Back his bright look shineth still

Whose keen glory with the night
Makes the lovely gray twilight,
Drawing out the downy owl,
With his musical bird-howl ;
Drawing out the leathery bats —
Mice they are, turned airy cats—
Noiseless, sly, and slippery things,
Swimming through the air on wings ;
Drawing out the feathery moth,
Lazy, drowsy, very loath :
She by daylight never flits—
Sleeps and nurses her five wits;
Drawing light from glowworms' tails,
Glimmering green in grassy dales;
Drawing children to the door,
For one goodnight-frolic more.

Then the moon comes up the hill,
Wide awake, but dreaming still ;

Soft and slow, as if in fear
Lest her path should not be clear,
Like a timid lady she
Looks around her daintily,
Begs the clouds to come about her,
Tells the stars to shine without her ;
But when we are lying like dead,
Sleeping in God's summer-bed,
She unveiled and bolder grown
Climbs the steps of her blue throne,
Stately in a calm delight,
Mistress of a whole fair night,
Drawing dreams, lovely and wild,
Out of father, mother, child.

But what fun is all about,
When the humans are shut out !
Night is then a dream opaque,
Full of creatures wide awake !

Noiseless then on feet or wings,

Out they come, all moon-eyed things !

Mice creep out of cracks in boles ;

I don't know—but mayn't the moles

Come up stairs to open their eyes?

Stars peep from their holes in the skies ;—

There they sparkle, pop, and play—

Have it all their own wild way ;

Fly and frolic, scamper, glow—

Treat the moon, for all her show,

State, and opal diadem,

Like a nursemaid watching them.

  'Tis the sun both day and night,

Shining here, or out of sight—

'Tis, I say, that fire of his

Makes the summer what it is.

He, across dividing fate

Seeks the moon disconsolate.

Like a lonely lady high
In a turret of the sky ;
Comforts her with comfort such
That she gives us her too-much.
Even when all his light is gone,
Still his warmth is working on,
With a hidden gentle might
Stretching summer through the night.—

 But the nightingale—ah, rare !
Turns it all, mighty and fair,
To a diamond hoop of song,
Which he trundles all night long.—

 When I heard him last, he sang
That the woody echoes rang—
Loud the secret out did call
In a wordless madrigal :
Through the early summer wood,
All the creatures understood.

What without a word he spoke,

I will tell the older folk,

Making it articulate,

Less divine and more sedate :

Here's the song the creatures heard

From the tiny, mighty bird :

Beautiful mother is busy all day—

So busy she neither can sing nor say ;

But lovely thoughts, in a ceaseless flow,

Through her eyes, and her ears, and her bosom go—

Motion, sight, and sound, and scent,

Weaving a royal, rich content.—

But when night is come, and her children sleep,

And beautiful mother her watch would keep—

With glowing stars in her dusky hair,

Down she sits to her music rare ;

And her instrument that never fails,

Is the hearts and the throats of her nightingales.

THE MISTLETOE.

Kiss me, kiss me, little Neddy.
—Ah, you see her, staring steady !
You have caught the pretty cheater
Sitting on her nest !   A neater
Never bird built on this planet—
Never was a sweeter than it ;
Never brood was such as this is :
That's the nest of all the kisses.
That's the kissing-bird—she's sitting
For the Christmas—never flitting—
Kisses, kisses, kisses hatching—
Sweetest birdies, for the catching.

THE MISTLETOE.

There ! that's one I caught this minute,
Musical as any linnet.
Where it is, your big eyes question—
With a doubt in their suggestion ?
There it is—upon mouth merry ;
There it is—upon cheek cherry ;
There's another on chin-chinnie ;
Now it's off, and lights on Minnie !
There's another on nose-nosey ;
There's another on lip-rosy ;
And the kissing-bird is hatching
Hundreds more, for only catching.

Why the mistletoe she chooses,
And the Christmas-tree refuses ?
There's a puzzle for your mother ?
I'll present you with another !—
Tell me, you cross-question-asker !
Cruel, heartless mother-tasker !

Why the wren should choose an apple;

Why jackdaw with beadles grapple:

Does he build in windy steeple,

To be near the praying people?

Will his Jacks be good daws for it?

Better sing, taught in church-turret?

Why the limping, cheating plover

O'er moist meadow likes to hover;

Why the partridge, with such trouble,

Builds her nest where soon the stubble

Will betray her hop-thumb-cheepers

To the eyes of all the reapers.—

Tell me, Charley; tell me, Janey;

Answer all—or answer any,

And I'll tell you, with much pleasure,

Why this little bird of treasure

Nestles only in the mistletoe,

Never, never goes the thistle to.

THE MISTLETOE.

Not an answer? Nought about it?
Then I'll answer you without it.
—Mistletoe will never flourish—
Find the life its life to nourish—
But on other plant well planted—
And for kissing two are wanted.
Therefore 'tis, the Kissing-birdie
Chooses not the oak-tree sturdie,
But the plant that grows upon it,
Like an As-you-like-it sonnet.

But, my blessed little mannie,
All the birdies are not cannie
That the Kissing-birdie hatches.
Some are worthless little patches—
Have no life in them to speak of—
Dead and gone your very cheek off!
Others leave such spots behind them,
On your cheek for years you find them.

—It depends what kind of net you
Set to catch one.   It will fret you
If you catch a winged mole, or
Any other flying crawler :
You won't like it, little Neddy ;
Therefore, sir, be wise and steady.
Kisses vain and kisses greedy,
Kisses careless, kisses needy,
Are as poor and mean and empty
As your favourite Humpty Dumpty
After his tremendous tumble,
Shedding brains it could not jumble :
May such kisses never touch you,
For they only smear and smutch you !
But the true heart seldom misses ;
That's the true net for true kisses !
Catch such birds—if once you catch them,
They are yours—you need not watch them.

WHAT PROFESSOR OWL *KNOWS*

NOBODY knows the world but me.

The rest go to bed : I sit up to see.

I'm a better student than any of you all,

For I never begin till the darkness fall,

And I never read without my glasses ;

But that's not how my wisdom passes.

I have learning, I say—but that's not it :

I observe.   I have seen the white moon sit

On her nest, the sea, like a second owl,

Hatching the boats and the long-legged fowl!

When the oysters gape—you may make a note—

She drops a pearl into every throat.

I can see the wind : now can you do that?
I see the dreams he carries in his hat ;
I see him snorting them out as he goes ;
I see them rush in at the snoring nose.
Ten thousand things you could not *think*,
I can write them down with pen and ink.

You see I know : you may pull off your hat,
Whether round and lofty, or square and flat.
You cannot do better than trust in me ;
You may shut your eyes in fact—*I* see.
Lifelong I will lead you, and then—I'm the owl--
I will bury you nicely with my spade and shovl.

WHAT THE BIRDS SAID AND WHAT THE BIRDS SUNG.

"I WILL sing a song:
  I'm the owl."

"Sing a song, you sing-song,
  Ugly fowl!
What will you sing about,
Night in and day out?"

"Sing about the night:
  I'm the owl."

"You could not see for the light,
  Stupid fowl!"

"Oh, the moon! and the dew!
And the shadows!—tu-whoo!"

" I will sing a song :
  I'm the nightingale."
" Sing a song, long, long.
  Little Neverfail !
What will you sing about,
Day in or day out ? "

" Sing about the light
  Gone away ;
Down, away, and out of sight :—
  Wake up, day !
For the day is not dead,
Only gone to bed."

————————————.

" I will sing a song :
  I'm the lark."
" Sing, sing, Throat-strong,
  Little Kill-the-dark !

WHAT THE BIRDS SAID.

What will you sing about,
Day in and night out?"

" I can only call;
    I can't think.
Let me up—that's all—
    For a drink !
Thirsting all the long night—
Let me drink the light !"

R &

RIDDLES.

I.

I HAVE only one foot, but thousands of toes ;
My one foot stands, but never goes.
I have many arms, and they're mighty all—
But hundreds of fingers, large and small.
From the ends of my fingers my beauty grows.
I breathe with my hair, and I drink with my toes.
I grow bigger and bigger about the waist,
And yet I am always very tight laced.
None e'er saw me eat—I've no mouth to bite—
Yet I eat all day in the full sunlight.
In the summer with song I shake and quiver;
But in winter I fast and groan and shiver.

II.

THERE is a plough that hath no share,
Only a coulter that parteth fair.

> But the ridges rise
> To a terrible size,

Or ever the coulter hath come to tear :
The horses and ridges fierce battle make ;
The horses are safe ; but the plough will break.

And the seed that is dropt in its furrows, I fear
Will lift to the sun neither blade nor ear ;

> For down it drops plumb,
> Where no spring-times come ;

Nor needeth it any harrowing gear.
Wheat nor poppy nor any leaf
Will cover this naked ground of grief.

BABY.

WHERE did you come from, baby dear ?
Out of the everywhere into here.

Where did you get those eyes so blue ?
Out of the sky as I came through.

What makes the light in them sparkle and spin ?
Some of the starry spikes left in.

Where did you get that little tear ?
I found it waiting when I got here.

What makes your forehead so smooth and high
A soft hand stroked it as I went by.

What makes your cheek like a warm white rose?
I saw something better than any one knows.

Whence that three-cornered smile of bliss?
Three angels gave me at once a kiss.

Where did you get this pearly ear?
God spoke, and it came out to hear.

Where did you get those arms and hands?
Love made itself into bonds and bands.

Feet, whence did you come, you darling things?
From the same box as the cherubs' wings.

How did they all just come to be you?
God thought about me, and so I grew.

But how did you come to us, you dear?
God thought about you, and so I am here.

UP AND DOWN.

THE sun is gone down,
  And the moon's in the sky;
But the sun will come up,
  And the moon be laid by.

The flower is asleep,
  But it is not dead;
When the morning shines,
  It will lift its head.

When winter comes,
  It will die—no, no:
It will only hide
  From the frost and snow.

UP AND DOWN.

Sure is the summer,
 Sure is the sun ;
The night and the winter—
 Away they run !

UP IN THE TREE.

WHAT would you see, if I took you up
    My little aerie-stair?
You would see the sky like a clear blue cup
    Turned upside down in the air.

What would you do, up my aerie-stair,
    In my little nest on the tree?
My child with cries would trouble the air,
    To get what she could but see.

What would you get in the top of the tree,
    For all your crying and grief?
Not a star would you clutch of all you see—
    You could only gather a leaf.

But when you had lost your greedy grief,
   Content to see from afar,
You would find in your hand a withering leaf,
   In your heart a shining star.

A BABY SERMON.

THE lightning and thunder
   They go and they come ;
But the stars and the stillness
   Are always at home.

LITTLE BO-PEEP.

LITTLE Bo-Peep, she lost her sheep,
　　And did not know where to find them :
They were over the height and out of sight,
　　Trailing their tails behind them.

Little Bo-Peep woke out of her sleep,
　　Jump'd up and set out to find them :
" The silly things ! they've got no wings,
　　And they've left their trails behind them :

" They've taken their tails, but they've left their
　　　　trails,
　　And so I shall follow and find them ; "
For wherever a tail had dragged a trail,
　　The long grass grew behind them ;

And day's eyes and butter-cups, cow's lips and
 Were shining in the sun :   [crow's feet
She threw down her book, and caught up her crook,
 And after her sheep did run.

She ran, and she ran, and ever as she ran,
 The grass grew higher and higher ;
Till over the hill the sun began
 To set in a flame of fire.

She ran on still—up the grassy hill,
 And the grass grew higher and higher.—
When she reached its crown, the sun was down,
 And had left a trail of fire.

The sheep and their tails were gone, all gone—
 And no more trail behind them !
Yes, yes—they were there—long-tailed and fair !
 But, alas, she could not find them !

Purple and gold, and rosy and blue,
  With their tails all white behind them,
Her sheep they did run in the trail of the sun :
  She saw them, but could not find them.

After the sun, like clouds they did run,
  But she knew they were her sheep :
She sat down to cry and look up at the sky,
  But she cried herself to sleep.

And as she slept the dew fell fast,
  And the wind blew from the sky ;
And strange things took place, that shun the day
  They are so sweet and shy.   [face—

Nibble, nibble, crop ! she heard as she woke :
  A hundred little lambs
Did pluck and eat the grass so sweet
  That grew in the trails of their dams.

Little Bo-Peep she caught up her crook,
    And wiped the tears that did blind her;
And nibble-nibble-crop! without a stop,
    The lambs came eating behind her.

Home, home she came, both tired and lame,
    With three times as many sheep.
In a month or more, they'll be as big as before,
    And then she'll laugh in her sleep.

But what would you say, if one fine day,
    When they've got their bushiest tails,
Their grown-up game should be just the same,
    And she have to follow their trails?

Never weep, Bo-Peep, though you lose your
    And do not know where to find them; [sheep,
'Tis after the sun the mothers have run,
    And there are the lambs behind them!

LITTLE BOY BLUE.

LITTLE Boy Blue lost his way in a wood—
    Sing apples and cherries, roses and honey .
He said, " I would not go back if I could,
    It's all so jolly and funny."

He sang, " This wood is all my own—
    Apples and cherries, roses and honey ;
Here I will sit, like a king on my throne,
    All so jolly and funny."

A little snake crept out of a tree—
    Apples and cherries, roses and honey :
" Lie down at my feet, little snake," said he—
    All so jolly and funny.

A little bird sang in the tree overhead—
 " *Apples and cherries, roses and honey :*"
" Come and sing your song on my finger instead,
 All so jolly and funny."   .

Up coiled the snake ; and the bird flew down,
And sang him the song of Birdie Brown.

But little Boy Blue found it tiresome to sit,
And he thought he had better walk on a bit.

So up he got, his way to take,
And said, "Come along, little bird and snake."

And waves of snake o'er the damp leaves passed
And the snake went first, and Birdie Brown last.

By Boy Blue's head, with flutter and dart,
Flew Birdie Brown, with its song in its heart.

He came where the apples grew red and sweet:
" Tree, drop me an apple down at my feet."

He came where the cherries hung plump and red :
" Come to my mouth, sweet kisses," he said.

And the boughs bow down, and the apples they
     dapple
The grass, too many for him to grapple.

And the cheeriest cherries, with never a miss,
Fall to his mouth, each a full-grown kiss.

He met a little brook singing a song :
He said, " Little brook, you are going wrong ;

" You must follow me, follow me, follow, I say—
Do as I tell you, and come this way."

And the song-singing, sing-songing forest brook
Leaped from its bed and after him took—

Followed him, followed.   And pale and wan,
The dead leaves rustled as the water ran.

And every bird high up on the bough,
And every creature low down below,

He called, and the creatures obeyed his call,
Took their legs and their wings and followed him
        all ;

Squirrels that carried their tails like a sack,
Each on his own little humpy brown back ;

Householder snails, and slugs all tails,
And butterflies, flutterbies, ships all sails ;

And weasels, and ousels, and mice, and larks,
And owls, and rere-mice, and harkydarks,

All went running, and creeping, and flowing,
After the merry boy fluttering and going ;

The dappled fawns fawning, the fallow-deer follow-
    ing ;
The swallows and flies, flying and swallowing;

Cockchafers, henchafers, cockioli-birds,
Cockroaches, henroaches, cuckoos in herds.

The spider forgot, and followed him spinning,
And lost all his thread from end to beginning.

The gay wasp forgot his rings and his waist—
He never had made such undignified haste.

The dragon-flies melted to mist with their hurry-
    ing.
The mole in his moleskins left his barrowing, bur-
    rowing.

The bees went buzzing, so busy and beesy,
And the midges in columns, so upright and easy.

But Little Boy Blue was not content,
Calling for followers still as he went,

Blowing his horn, and beating his drum,
And crying aloud, ''Come all of you, come!''

He said to the shadows, ''Come after me;''
And the shadows began to flicker and flee;

And they flew through the wood all flattering and
     fluttering,
Over the dead leaves flickering and muttering.

And he said to the wind, ''Come, follow; come,
     follow,
With whistle and pipe, and rustle and hollo.''

And the wind wound round at his desire,
As if he had been the gold cock on the spire.

And the cock itself flew down from the church,
And left the farmers all in the lurch.

They run and they fly, they creep and they come,
Everything, everything, all and some.

The very trees they tugged at their roots,
Only their feet were too fast in their boots,

After him leaning and straining and bending,
As on through their boles he kept walking and
      wending;

Till out of the wood he burst on a lea,
Shouting and calling, "Come after me!"

And then they rose with a leafy hiss,
And stood as if nothing had been amiss.

Little Boy Blue sat down on a stone,
And the creatures came round him every one.

And he said to the clouds, "I want you there!"
And down they sank through the thin blue air.

And he said to the sunset far in the west,
" Come here; I want you; I know best."

And the sunset came and stood up on the wold,
And burned and glowed in purple and gold.

Then Little Boy Blue began to ponder:
" What's to be done with them all, I wonder."

Then Little Boy Blue, he said, quite low,
" What to do with you all, I am sure I don't know."

Then the clouds clodded down till dismal it grew;
The snake sneaked close; round Birdie Brown flew;

The brook sat up like a snake on its tail;
And the wind came up with a *what-will-you* wail;

And all the creatures sat and stared ;
The mole opened his very eyes and glared ;

And for rats and bats, and the world and his wife,
Little Boy Blue was afraid of his life.

Then Birdie Brown began to sing,
And what he sang was tne very thing :

'You have brought us all hither, Little Boy
     Blue :
Pray what do you want us all to do ? "

"Go away ; go away ; " said Little Boy Blue ;
"I'm sure I don't want you—get away—do."

"No, no ; no, no ; no, yes, and no, no,"
Sang Birdie Brown—"it mustn't be so.

"We cannot for nothing come here, and away.
Give us some work, or here we stay."

They covered the earth, and they darkened the air;
They hovered, and sat—with a countless stare !

If he did not give them something to do,
They might stare him up, for what he knew.

" Oh dear! and oh dear ! " with sob and with sigh,
Said Little Boy Blue, and began to cry.

But he had not cried long till he thought of a thing ;
And up he stood, and spoke like a king :

" Why do you hustle and jostle and bother ?
Off with you all !   Take me back to my mother."

The sunset stood at the gates of the west.
" Follow *me*, follow *me*," came from Birdie
　　　　Brown's breast.

" I am going that way as fast as I can,"
Said the brook, as it sank and turned and ran.

Back to the woods fled the shadows like ghosts :
"If we stay, we shall all be missed from our posts."

Said the wind with a voice that had changed its
    cheer,
"I was just going there, when you brought me
    here."

" 'That's where I live," said the sack-backed
    squirrel,
And he turned his sack with a swing and a swirl.

Said the cock of the spire: " His father's church-
    warden."
Said the brook, running faster, "I run through
    his garden."

Said the mole, " Two hundred worms—there I
    caught 'em
Last year, and I'm going again next autumn."

Said they all, "If that's where you want us to
　　　　steer for,
What on earth or in air did you bring us here for?"

"Never you mind," said Little Boy Blue;
"That's what I tell you.　If that you won't do,

"I'll get up at once, and go home without you.
—I think I will : I begin to doubt you."

He rose.　Then uprose the snake on its tail,
And hissed three times, a hiss full of bale,

And shot out his tongue at Boy Blue to scare him.
He turned to pass, but the snake turned to dare
　　　　him.

Boy Blue got angry : "You snake," he said,
　'Get out of my way, or I'll break your head."

The snake he neither would go nor come ;
Boy Blue hit him hard with the stick of his drum.

The snake fell down as if he was dead,
And Little Boy Blue set his foot on his head.

" Hurrah ! " cried the creatures — " Hurray
        Hurrah !
Little Boy Blue, your will is a law ! "

And round they turned and marched before him,
And marshalled him home with a high cockolorum.

And Birdie Brown sang, " *Twirrr twitter, twirr*
        tweee !
  In the rosiest rose-bush a rare nest !
Twirr twitter, twirrr twitter, twirrr twitter,
        twirrrrr tweeeee !
  In the fun he has found the earnest ! "

WILLIE'S QUESTION.

I.

Willie speaks.

Is it wrong to wish to be great,
   For I do wish it so?
I have asked already my sister Kate ;
   She says she does not know.

This morning a trumpet blast
   Made all my room to quake ;
It came so sudden and shook so fast,
   It blew me wide awake.

It told me I must make haste,
   And some great glory win ;
For every day was running to waste :
   I must at once begin.

To-night at the gate I stood,
   Watching the sun set slow ;
When I saw him look so grand and good,
   It came with a purple glow.

And next from the shining moon
   It stole like a silver dart.
When the wind began his stormy tune,
   It woke with a sudden start.

I want to be great and strong ;
   I want to begin to-day ;
But if you think it very wrong,
   I will send the wish away.

II.

The Father answers.

Is it wrong to wish to be great?
  No, Willie; it is not wrong:
The child who stands at the high closed gate,
  Must wish to be tall and strong.

If you did not wish to grow,
  I should be a sorry man;
I should think my boy was dull and slow,
  And unworthy of his clan.

You are bound to be great, my boy:
  Wish, and get up, and do.
Were you content to be little, my joy
  Would be little enough in you.

WILLIE'S QUESTION.

Willie speaks.

Papa, papa ! I'm so glad
    That what I wish is right !
I will not lose a chance to be had ;
    I'll begin this very night.

I will work so hard at school,
    And give no time to play !
At my fingers' ends I'll have every rule—
    For knowledge is power, they say.

I *would* be a king and reign;
    But I can't be that—and so—
Field-marshal I'll be, I think—and gain
    Sharp battles and sieges slow.

I shall gallop and shout and call,
    Waving my shining sword :

Cavalry, infantry, officers, all
    Hear and obey my word.

Or admiral I will be—
    Wherever the salt wave runs,
Sailing, fighting over the sea,
    With flashing and roaring guns.

I will make myself hardy and strong,
    And be brave, and never give in.
I *am* so glad it is not wrong,
    And at once I will begin !

The Father speaks.

Fighting and shining along,
    All for the show of the thing !
Any puppet will mimic the grand and strong
    If you pull the proper string !

Willie speaks.

But if I could be great,
  I should not mind the show ;
For what I want is the glory-state—
  Above the rest, you know.

The Father answers.

The harder you run that race,
  The farther you tread that track,
The greatness you fancy before your face
  Is the farther behind your back.

To be up in the heavens afar,
  Miles above all the rest,
Will make no star the greatest star—
  Only the dreariest.

That book on the higher shelf
  Is not therefore the greater book ;

If you would be great, it must be in yourself,
   And neither by place nor look.

The Highest is not high
   By being higher than others.
To greatness you come not a step more nigh
   By getting above your brothers.

III.

Willie speaks.

I MEANT the boys at school —
   I did not mean my brother.
i suppose somebody must have the rule—
   As well be me as another.

The Father answers.

Oh, Willie ! it's all the same ;
   They are your brothers ai₄ ,

For when you say, "Hallowed be thy name,"
   Whose Father is it you call?

Could you pray for such rule to *him?*
   Do you think that he would hear?
Must he favour one in a greedy whim,
   When all are his children dear?

It is right to get up and do;
   But why outstrip the rest?
Why should one of the many be one of the few?
   Why should *you* think to be best?

Willie speaks.

Then how am I to be great?
   I know no other way.
It will not answer to sit and wait;
   I must up and do, you say.

The Father answers.

I do not want you to wait ;
  For few before they die
Have got so far as begin to be great—
  The lesson is so high.

I will tell you the only plan
  To climb and not to fall:
He who would be the greatest man
  Must be the servant of all.

If you turn other ways your mind—
  To work on some shining plan,
You may think you are great, but will come
    to find
  You are not even a man.

Climb to the top of the trees,
   Climb to the top of the hill,
Get up on the crown of the sky if you please,
   You'll be a small creature still.

Be admiral, poet, or king,
   Let praises fill both your ears,
Your soul will be but a windmill thing
   Blown round by its hopes and fears.

IV.

Willie speaks.

THEN put me in the way,
   For you, papa, are a man:
What thing shall I do this very day?—
   Only be sure I *can.*

I want to know—I am willing—
 I would not leave it to chance:
Shall I give the monkey-boy my shilling?—
 I want to serve at once.

The Father answers.

Give all your shillings you might,
 And hurt your brothers the more;
He only can serve his fellows right
 Who goes in at the little door.

We must do the thing we *must*
 Before the thing we *may*;
We are unfit for any trust
 Until we can obey.

Willie speaks.

I will not plague you more—
 Not one more question ask;

But you shall show me the little door ;
　You shall set me my task.

The Father answers.

No, Willie ; the Father of all,
　Teacher and Master high,
Has set your task beyond recall,
　And you cannot set it by.

I do not know your task ;
　I am only a child, like you ;
I can only urge you, when you ask,
　To listen and hear and do.

Willie speaks.

I hear him not, although
　1 am listening very strong ;
His voice must either be very low,
　Or up the clouds among.

The Father answers.

It is not hard to hear,
    And its words are very few ;
It is very low, but very near,
    And none can hear it but you.

Willie answers.

I do not hear it at all ;
    I am only hearing you.

The Father speaks.

Think : is there nothing, great or small,
    You ought to go and do ?

Willie answers.

Let me think :—I ought to feed
    My rabbits.   I went away

In such a hurry this morning !   Indeed
  They've not had enough to-day.

The Father speaks.

That is his whisper low !
  That is his very word !
You had only to stop and listen that so
  It might be plainly heard.

Willie, that duty's the door :
  You must open it and go in;
There is nothing else to do before ;
  There is nowhere else to begin.

Willie speaks.

But that's so easily done !
  It's such a trifling affair !
It is almost over as soon as begun :
  For that he can hardly care.

The Father answers.

As long as you linger and wait,
  You are turning from his call :
It is because you are not great,
  You think any duty small.

One at a time, and no more ;
  The nearest first to begin :
What matter how little the little door,
  If it only lets you in ?

*   *   *   *

V.

Willie speaks.

PAPA, I am come again.
  It is now three months and more
That I've tried to do the thing that was plain,
  But I feel as small as before.

The Father answers.

Your honour comes too slow ?
  How much then have you done ?
One foot on a mole-heap, would you crow
  As if you had reached the sun ?

Willie speaks.

But I begin to doubt
  Whether this way be the true ;
For the more you do to work it out,
  The more there seems to do.

I am sure, when all is past,
   I shall feel no greater so;
For if I had done the very last—
   It was but my duty, you know.

It is only much the same
   As not being liar or thief.

The Father answers.

One who tried it, found even, with shame,
   That of sinners he was the chief.

My boy, I am glad indeed!
   You have been discovering!

Willie speaks.

But then, papa, I shall never speed:
   Whence is my greatness to spring?

WILLIE'S QUESTION.

If duty itself must fail—
    And that be the only plan—
How shall my blundering failure prevail
    To make me a mighty man ?

The Father answers.

Ah, Willie! what if it were
    Quite another way to fall ?
What if the greatness itself lay there—
    In knowing that you are small ?

In seeing the good so good
    That you feel poor, weak, and low ;
And hungrily long for it as for food,
    With an endless need to grow ?

The man who was lord of fate,
    Born in an ox's stall,
Was great because he was too great
    To care about greatness at all.

Ever and only he sought
　　The will of his Father good :
Never of what was high he thought,
　　But of what his Father would.

You long to be great ; you try ;
　　You feel yourself smaller still :
In the name of God let ambition die ·
　　Let him make you what he will

Who does the truth, is one
　　With the living Truth above :
Be God's obedient little son,
　　And ambition will die in love.

END OF VOL. II'